GOOD ENOUGH

JEN PETRO-ROY

SQUARE
FISH

FEIWEL AND FRIENDS
NEW YORK

ALSO BY JEN PETRO-ROY

P.S. I Miss You

You Are Enough

———

SQUARE FISH

An imprint of Macmillan Publishing Group, LLC
120 Broadway, New York, NY 10271
mackids.com

GOOD ENOUGH. Copyright © 2019 by Jen Petro-Roy.
All rights reserved. Printed in the United States of America
by LSC Communications, Harrisonburg, Virginia.

Square Fish and the Square Fish logo are trademarks of Macmillan and
are used by Feiwel and Friends under license from Macmillan.

Our books may be purchased in bulk for promotional, educational, or business use.
Please contact your local bookseller or the Macmillan Corporate and Premium
Sales Department at (800) 221-7945 ext. 5442 or by email at
MacmillanSpecialMarkets@macmillan.com.

Names: Petro-Roy, Jen, author.
Title: Good enough / Jen Petro-Roy.
Description: First edition. | New York : Feiwel and Friends, 2019. |
Summary: In the hospital where she is receiving treatment for anorexia,
twelve-year-old Riley records her days in her journal—going to therapy,
rediscovering her love of art, dealing with her rule-breaking roommate,
and worrying about relapse once she returns home.
Identifiers: LCCN 2018020004 | ISBN 978-1-250-23350-9 (paperback) |
ISBN 978-1-250-12350-3 (ebook)
Subjects: | CYAC: Anorexia nervosa—Fiction. | Hospitals—Fiction. |
Friendship—Fiction. | Family life—Fiction. | Diaires—Fiction.
Classification: LCC PZ7.1.P473 Go 2019 | DDC [Fic]—dc23
LC record available at https://lccn.loc.gov/2018020004

Originally published in the United States by Feiwel and Friends
First Square Fish edition, 2020
Book designed by Liz Dresner
Square Fish logo designed by Filomena Tuosto

3   5   7   9   10   8   6   4

P9-DHL-238

*To the real Brenna and Ali, and
to everyone else I met along the way*

DAY ONE: MONDAY

There's a girl with an IV in the bed next to me. She's pale and has dark circles under her eyes, like she didn't get any sleep last night. She probably didn't. That's why she's sleeping now, at four in the afternoon.

I can't remember the last time I took a nap. Last year, maybe, when I had the flu and Mom made sure I was tucked into bed and wrapped in blankets. That's when Mom told me I was an awful napper as a baby. "You didn't sleep at night and you didn't nap during the day." She stifled a yawn as she said it, like when someone in school yawns and I do, too. I guess Mom's memory was contagious. "You fussed and cried until I had to take you out of your crib and strap you to my chest to get anything done." I like imagining myself in one of those baby-carrier things, as safe and cozy as a baby kangaroo.

I definitely don't feel safe and cozy right now.

IV Girl's eyelids just fluttered. I thought she was going to wake up. I'm not sure I *want* her to wake up. Well, I do *eventually*. I don't want her to *die*. But she can sleep a bit longer. I need to get used to this place first.

(I don't think I'll ever get used to this place.)

I wonder why this girl's on an IV. She could be dehydrated. That happened to my friend Emerson once when she didn't drink enough water at a track meet. But Emerson was fine after she chugged a bottle of grape Gatorade (the grossest kind). IV Girl must be really sick. Way sicker than me.

I don't know if that makes me relieved or disappointed.

I hope she's nice. I hope she likes me.

This hospital is cold. IV Girl has three blankets over her. I want to steal one to put over my legs, but that would *not* be a good first impression. Everyone would call me the Blanket Thief. They'd hide their stuff when I walked by. They'd hate me.

Not that I should care about first impressions. I shouldn't care about IV Girl liking me, either. I'm not going to be here long enough to make friends. I'm never going to see anyone here after today. Maybe after *tomorrow*, if it takes that long to convince them I don't belong in the hospital.

The phone's ringing in the hallway. It's rung about seventy times since I got here, which was only a half hour ago. I hear footsteps outside, too, shuffling ones and stomping ones. The creak of a cart. Someone yelling. I won't look, though. I'll stare out the window and write in my journal, even though all I want to do is hide my head under this limp pillow and cry until *I* fall asleep, too.

I can't let myself cry. That's what Mom wants me to do. She wants me to collapse in exhaustion and admit I need help. She wants me to admit I'm sad and hungry and tired. To let other people feed me like I'm a baby and they're waiting with a spoonful of mushed peas.

Mushed peas are gross. Food is gross.

Mom thinks that once I'm locked behind these doors, everything's going to be all right. Like they can give me a magic pill, or a course of antibiotics with the side effect of "recovery." Things will go back to normal and I'll be the old Riley again.

I don't know who "the old Riley" *is* anymore, though. And there are no antibiotics that will get rid of my thoughts, which are way too powerful to be silenced. They tell me I'm not good enough. They tell me to be skinnier and prettier. To run more and eat less.

They tell me that everything about me is wrong.

Those thoughts are part of me now. These people here, the doctors and the nurses and the counselors and the nutritionists— they can't take them away. I don't want them to take them away.

I'd be fat then.

I don't want to be fat.

Then I'd be nothing at all.

———

I bet it's loud here at night. I bet there's screaming and crying and people running up and down the hallway having nervous breakdowns. Mean nurses who yell at you for breathing too loudly.

Strangers from other floors wandering into the rooms. I'll find out tonight, I guess.

I keep hoping Mom's going to realize she made a big mistake and—*SCREECH!*—veer her car onto the exit ramp of the highway, turn around, and bring me home.

Mom wouldn't do that, though. Mom's a good driver. She doesn't *ever* screech. She barely goes the speed limit. Plus, I bet she has a meeting this afternoon with some hotshot artist who wants to display in her gallery. Or a collection of sculptures she needs to dust. Screeching around would take up valuable time.

I don't get Mom's valuable time anymore. She doesn't think I deserve it.

I'm *not* selfish, though. When Mom called me selfish, I felt sick. My stomach felt like it did that time I was playing kickball and Julia whaled the ball into my gut. I gasped for air and almost puked up my Cheerios. Julia ran around the bases and did that annoying victory dance where she wiggles her butt.

(Butts are the height of eleven-year-old humor. Actually, butts are the height of guy-in-my-seventh-grade-class humor, too.)

I'm not doing this for attention, though. I don't *want* attention like this. I would have been fine if no one had noticed what I was doing. I would have been *so* fine. I would have been *perfect* if Mom hadn't noticed me. After all, she usually doesn't.

Then she did. And she and Dad sent me here.

IV Girl is making little moaning noises, like she's hovering on the edge of a nightmare. She looks really sick; her skin is pale and her cheekbones look like the topographical map Mr. Baldwin has on the table in the back of his classroom. Two cheek mountains, sharper and steeper than Mount Everest.

I wonder how much she weighs. I wonder how much I weigh. Mom didn't let me get on the scale this morning. She hid it last week, but I found it right away, on the top shelf of the linen closet. Mom's never been good at hiding things. She still hides my Christmas presents under a blanket in the basement. (Have some imagination, lady.)

Mom was my shadow from the second I woke up this morning, though. I bet she thought I was going to run away. I wish I *had* run away.

"I'm okay, Mom." She had one hand on my shoulder, her fingernails as sharp as an eagle's talons. I was the mouse, wriggling to get free. "I'm fine. I don't need to go to the hospital. You can go to work today. I'll eat, I promise."

(I wasn't going to eat.)

"You're *not* going to eat," Mom said. "You had your chance, and I already took the day off. You need help, Riley." Dad nodded sternly, backing Mom up. That's all he's been doing lately, nodding and pressing his lips together like he's a reality TV judge making a "very important decision." He's barely said a word to me since they figured everything out. Just "excuse me" when he walks

5

by me on the way to the bathroom or "bring your umbrella" when it looks like it's going to rain.

You know, quality father-daughter stuff.

Julia poked her head out of her room, then tiptoed out on her skinny legs. She already had her backpack on and her hair was in a tight French braid. As usual, not a strand was out of place and the sides were slicked back with hair spray and bobby pins. Once, we counted the bobby pins after one of her gymnastic meets. She'd used thirty-five! Dad joked that he should buy stock in hair products. Mom grumped that maybe then she wouldn't have to work so much to pay gymnastics tuition.

They'd never make Julia stop gymnastics, though. Even if Mom and Dad have to get three extra jobs each. Even if Dad has to pick up trash on the side of the road and Mom has to empty porta potties (which is probably the grossest job in the history of the universe). Julia's too good. She has too much "potential."

Potential. I hate that word. Potential is what Julia has when she's swinging through the air like she's close enough to grasp a star from the sky. Potential is what Emerson and my nemesis, Talia, have when they're sprinting down the straightaway during track meets, their arms pumping as they gain that last bit of speed.

Potential is what everyone has. Everyone but me. I'm the boring one. The one whose life is about to be ruined forever.

I bet Julia feels sorry for me. That's why she couldn't look me in the eye. Mom says Julia's scared, even though I keep telling my family that there's nothing to be scared about.

That I'm just doing the same things the other kids at school do.

That I'm not too skinny.

That I can stop whenever I want to. (I just don't want to yet.)

"Good luck, Riley." Julia's voice trembled when she said good-bye this morning. She looked as nervous as I felt, so I forced myself to smile. Mom and Dad didn't tell Julia I was going away until last night. They sprang it on her during dinner, like a lion leaping out of a clump of grass. Except instead of being attacked with claws and sharp teeth, Julia got attacked with the news that her older sister was going to the hospital.

She cried for five minutes straight. Mom looked at me like *I* was supposed to make Julia feel better, like the crying was my fault, too. *Everything* is my fault now. Meanwhile Dad just sat there eating his mashed potatoes. Of course neither of *them* admitted that waiting until the last minute to tell Julia may have been a bad idea. Nope, not Mom and Dad. They're probably preparing their Parents of the Year speeches already. They can hang their blue ribbons next to Julia's overflowing collection in the spare bedroom.

This *has* to be a quick stay. I'm not *that* sick. I eat. I just don't eat as much as Mom and Dad want me to. This is so unfair. I definitely don't look as bad as IV Girl.

She's awake. She just looked at me. Blinked twice, then rolled over.

Does IV Girl hate me already? Is she like Talia and all her friends, who act like X-ray machines searching me for anything—everything—defective?

I bet she snores, too.

———

Mom didn't come back. It's been an hour since I last wrote and she still hasn't come back. I didn't think she *really* would, but I was "pretend" hoping, like when I asked Santa for a unicorn for Christmas. I knew he wouldn't *really* get me a unicorn, but I asked anyway, just in case. I still held my breath going down the stairs on Christmas morning.

I wasn't *that* disappointed, but I was a little bit disappointed.

A unicorn would have been the coolest present.

Getting out of here would be even better.

———

IV Girl's name is Ali. She's twelve, like me, and she's from Missouri. She flew three hours to get here. Apparently this is a "really good program."

"Translation: it will make us really fat," Ali whispered, even though there were no nurses or counselors around. Jean, the nurse who'd done my orientation, had gone to "get something." She still isn't back. I guess "somethings" are hard to find. I'm okay with that, though. Jean makes me nervous, like if I breathe the wrong way, she'll lock me in solitary confinement.

This whole place feels like solitary confinement. Like we're lab animals shut up in a box and part of some big experiment.

Let's see what happens to Subject Riley when we stuff her full of calories! Then a sadistic doctor will rub his hands together and let out an evil laugh. *BWAHAHAHA!*

At least we have windows in our room. Big, long ones that fill up the whole wall. I can see the sky and the sun and a bird flitting between two trees. It's nice outside, even though it feels like the world should be crying with me. That the tulips in the garden below should be black and gray instead of red and orange.

The comforter on this bed is as thin as a sheet, and the sheets feel like they have sand sprinkled all over them. I bet I'll get a rash. Or bedbugs. I already feel itchy.

———

Ali's been here for a week already. She has anorexia, like me.

I have anorexia. That's weird to write. I've never thought about it like that before, but that's what Mom says I have. That's what Dad *would* say I have if he actually talked to me about what's going on. That's what the admission people say I have. *Anorexia nervosa*: they wrote it in red pen on the top of my file.

I don't *feel* like I have a disease. I'm not barfing or fainting. Well, I almost fainted that one time at school, but that was just once. One fainting spell does not make me sick. *Especially* since I feel ridiculously huge. I didn't run today. All I've been doing is sitting. In the car. In the waiting room. In this room. I want to move, but I can't. They won't let me.

"We can't exercise and we eat basically all day long." Ali tapped the bag on her IV stand. It swung like a pendulum. "I have to be hooked up to this thing all the time, too. More nutrients. More fluids." She pretended to gag. "They're inflating me like a balloon. It's the worst." She smiled. It was a tiny smile, but it was definitely a smile.

Maybe Ali doesn't hate me. Maybe she's just a grump when she wakes up. Josie's like that at sleepovers. She grumbles and moans if she gets up before eight a.m. She's crabby in homeroom, too.

Ali's smile is crooked, like Emerson's, except Emerson's mouth turns up on the left side and Ali's does on the right.

Emerson smiled when we said good-bye yesterday, but I could tell it was forced. She joked about how jealous she was that I'd get to eat so much yummy food. How I probably planned this so I could skip track practice.

I don't *want* to skip track practice. I don't want to eat, either. I told Emerson that. "Mom's making a big deal out of things." I rolled my eyes. "You know how she is, always overreacting." Mom does overreact. Whenever she gets a sniffle, she pops zinc cough drops and drinks fortified orange juice like it's her job.

Which it's not. As far as I know, gallery owners don't run on orange juice. They run on Fitbits and buzzing iPhones and Pilates classes. Oh, and meetings. Lots and lots of meetings.

I keep tapping my foot and jiggling my leg. It's the closest thing to running I can get. Track practice ends around now. The other girls are probably changing out of their sweaty clothes, chugging water, and breaking into their post-workout snack stashes. I'd be on the track still, running extra laps, yelling an excuse to Emerson when she invited me over after practice.

Then I'd run some more. To get better. To lose more weight.

Emerson said she'd call me tonight. Or e-mail me tomorrow.

Josie hasn't said anything to me since last week.

———

Ali talks a lot. Everyone here does. Jean blabbed on and on about the rules while she helped me unpack.

No outside food.

No exercise.

No visitors outside of weekends and evening hours unless they're approved.

Participate.

Be honest.

Eat according to your meal plan.

I'm glad Jean didn't make me sign an agreement, because there's no *way* I can agree to those rules. I'll eat, but I'll only eat so I can get out of here faster. And I *won't* be honest. They don't need to know about my feelings.

I'll smile and nod until my head falls off.

That will be my disguise.

I have to go eat dinner now.

I don't want to eat dinner now.

———

I ate dinner.

An entire "my plate is full and I'll get in trouble if I don't eat it" meal.

I ate everything.

My stomach hurts so much. It looks like there's a baby in there.

We had a group after. That's what we do here. We eat and have groups and meet with therapists and nutritionists. We listen and tell the truth and share secrets and talk about how we *feel*. We gain weight.

My chest is seizing up. I want to go for a run. I need to go for a run. My times are dropping with every second I sit on my butt.

I'm already the slowest one on the team; I can't afford to get worse. I have to be in shape to qualify for regionals next month. I have to have to have to.

I'm trying to jiggle my leg so the counselor doesn't notice. That's *some* movement, at least.

The counselor noticed. She raised her eyebrows and pursed her lips, like that old lady who works at the pharmacy does every time she sees me. I bet she still thinks I'm a little kid who'll throw a tantrum if Mom doesn't give me the chocolate bar I asked for.

Hah! There's no way I'd ever ask for a chocolate bar.

I stopped jiggling. At least I didn't get in trouble. Maybe I got a free pass because it's my first day here. I still want to move, though. Why am I the only one freaking out? No one else looks like they're in pain. Why does my stomach hurt so much? Is there something wrong with me?

I can't write any more tonight. I can't think about this. Except I have snack soon. More food. Then I'll go to bed. So I can do this all over again tomorrow.

DAY TWO: TUESDAY

You know what the grossest rule of all is? The one that I couldn't even write down yesterday because I hoped they'd somehow change their minds? The counselors stand outside the bathroom while we pee. THEY LISTEN TO US PEE. (Poop, too, obviously, but I haven't done that yet.) They stand so close I can hear them loud-breathing through the door.

All the bathrooms are locked. Even the ones in our rooms. The nurses and counselors have keys and we have to *ask* them to go to the bathroom, like we're in preschool and need someone to wipe our butts. I wonder what happens when someone *really* has to go. Like emergency pee alert. What if they can't find a staff member in time? Ew.

They make us count while we're peeing, too. Out loud. They say it's so they know we're not throwing up. So our "vocal cords are occupied." Yesterday I stopped counting for a second to concentrate and Jean yelled at me. Is it my fault I have a shy bladder? I didn't end up going at all, and she looked at me like I was breaking the rules on purpose.

I'm *not*. I think Ali *is*, though.

I almost feel like I was dreaming this, but I think I heard Ali doing crunches last night. In her bed. At an eating disorder treatment center. The night counselor had just left after checking that we were "safe." I was trying (and failing) to fall asleep.

Then Ali's bed started creaking. I rolled over, then squeezed my eyes closed again. I didn't want Ali to know I was awake. Some light streamed in from the hallway, and the shadow in Ali's bed moved up and down. She gasped for breath a few times.

I tried not to move so she wouldn't realize I'd heard her. So the night nurse wouldn't hear *me*. We might both get in trouble then.

I wonder if they make us eat more food if we get in trouble. If they bring us to some secret room where there's a banquet table full of food: turkey and gravy and lasagna and five different kinds of cake. Soft, buttery crescent rolls and apple pies fresh out of the oven. Gingerbread men like Mom makes at Christmas and Grandma Archibald's famous mashed potatoes.

I think about food way too much. I don't want to like food. I can't help it, though. I tell myself I don't want the food they give us. I tell myself it's disgusting.

I still want it, though. I'm glad they're making me eat.

That banquet table would be my nightmare and my dream come true at the same time.

15

At least they're not weighing me today. They do that on Mondays, Wednesdays, and Fridays. "If we weighed you every day, you'd start obsessing over it," Jean explained yesterday. I couldn't tell if she was making a joke. I'm going to obsess over my weight no matter *how* often they weigh me. It's what I do. It's why I'm here.

Jean woke me and Ali up this morning. She poked her head in the door and flipped the light switch on and off three times. I was already awake, but it was still the most annoying thing ever. "Rise and shine, campers!" she exclaimed. "It's time to start another day!"

I'm surprised she wasn't wearing a Camp Eat-a-Lot shirt or a lanyard around her neck. I wonder if they make lanyards here. Ali says we do lots of arts and crafts. I'm kind of excited about that. Okay, not *excited* excited, but there's a bubbly feeling in my stomach at the thought of picking up markers and pencils again.

I think I might miss drawing. It's hard to write that, but I do. I used to draw a lot, but I haven't for a long time. I miss how fun coloring books were when I was a kid, when I was allowed to go outside the lines. I miss papier-mâché day in art class—getting my hands all glue-sticky and wiggling them in the air while Emerson and Josie shrieked and ran away. I miss sitting outside and creating on paper what I see with my eyes.

I *shouldn't* miss drawing, though, because I'm not good at it. And if I'm not good at it, I shouldn't do it. I don't do real art, not like the people Mom works with. I don't do modern art, with its bold colors and swirls that are supposed to mean something all deep and symbolic. I don't make fancy mobiles, like that famous guy who says they symbolize "the way society is forever spinning around." I tried to do landscapes and vases and ladies in fancy dresses, but something always looked wrong.

My trees aren't "regal" enough.

My shadowing is somehow off.

My noses are too pointy.

I'll never be able to do paintings like Mom shows in her gallery. And when I draw what I like, when I doodle faces and penguins and frogs with magic wands, they're childish. Boring. Normal.

I *could* be good at running, though, as long as I stay skinny. I could make regionals. Maybe I could even get a ribbon, too: a blue one, a red one, a yellow one . . . whatever. I just want something of my own. Something I'm good at. Running *has* to be it. I'm getting better every day.

Not today, though. I definitely can't run in here. I bet they'll barely let me *walk* in here. I'll sleep all night and sit all day, like a sloth. Like the slothiest sloth that's ever slothed.

Not running feels wrong. It makes my body feel wrong. My legs feel heavy, like they're weighed down. Like if I jumped into a pool, I'd sink to the very bottom.

I'd drown.

I'm scared. I shouldn't be scared, but I am.

"It's just food." That's what Dad says when he makes pancakes for breakfast and ends up screaming at me because I won't eat them. He doesn't get it, though. It's not just food. It's . . .

I can't explain it to Dad. I can't even explain it to myself. All I know is that the thought of eating a stack of puffy pancakes slathered with butter and syrup makes my entire body clench up. It makes my shoulders stiffen. It makes my stomach churn into a stormy ocean of water and Diet Coke.

Emerson doesn't get it, either. When I told her where I was going, her forehead got all wrinkly. "How can you not like food? Pizza is the best thing ever. It's heaven in circular form." That's Emerson, though. Emerson the *"naturally* skinny." Emerson the "doesn't *have* to run extra to stay in the right size pants."

I think my friend Josie kind of gets it. Well, she *did*, before she stopped talking to me. Talia used to make fun of Josie, too, for having so many pimples. Josie's cried about how she looks, too.

I've already cried three times today. I miss my friends. I miss home. I miss how things used to be.

I talked with one of the counselors before breakfast. Her name is Heather. She's always smiling and has this sickly sweet voice that makes me want to give her something sour to eat, just to balance things out. Heather told me their goal is for me to eat "normally" again.

There's that word again. *Normal.* Everyone's obsessed with it. Apparently I'm not normal because I don't like to eat breakfast. But neither does Mom. And no one's calling *her* sick and locking *her* up. Mom eats diet food, too. She weighs herself every day. No one sends *her* to treatment.

Julia doesn't snack much, either. That's because gymnasts have to be skinny and thin and willowy and every other possible synonym for *beautiful.* Julia's underweight, too. But people call *her* a superstar.

So why am *I* "abnormal"? What if not eating breakfast *is* normal for *me*? Didn't Mrs. Cashman tell us in kindergarten that we're all special, unique snowflakes? That we all have different talents and blah-de-blah-de-blah?

What if I *eat* like a special snowflake, too? But nope. No one considers *my* opinion. They tell me I'm starving myself. They say they're doing this to make me "healthy."

Healthy (adj.) Definition: Fat.

Heather said that fat isn't bad. That fat in food gives my hair shine and my body cushion. She says that it's not bad to *be* fat, either. That my body doesn't define me, and I can live a great life no matter what I look like.

I *know* that. I know that bodies come in all shapes and sizes.

19

I don't care about my friends' weights. I know there's nothing wrong with eating a lot. Or being fat.

I just don't want to be fat. I don't want to be normal, either.

Normal will turn me back into Roly-Poly Riley. Back the way I was before. It'll be like the Fairy Godmother scene in *Cinderella*, except instead of turning into a princess, things will be the other way around: *bibbidi-bobbidi-BLOB*.

I want to go home. I want to go to track practice before Coach Jackson kicks me off the team. He might anyway. He already yells that I'm "slow as molasses!" I can hear his raspy shout in my head right now.

If I get kicked off the team, I don't know what I'll do.

No. That *won't* happen. I'll get out, lose this weight, and be better than ever. I'll run more than usual to make up for the time I lost in here. I'll run all day long if I have to. I'll be good. Better. Best.

———

Ali keeps staring at me. She's acting like I'm a frog under a microscope and she's examining all my parts. I bet she knows I heard her last night. I bet she thinks I'm going to tell on her. I'd never do that, though. I'm not a tattletale.

What I am is jealous.

I'm also "medically compromised." That's the technical term

the admission guy used yesterday. His name was Bob. A boring name for a boring guy. He had brown hair in a buzz cut and boring brown glasses. Every time he asked me a question or said something to Mom, he spoke in a low, monotone voice. Like nothing exciting has ever happened to him and nothing ever will.

"Do you think you're sick?"

"What do you see when you look in the mirror?"

"What have you eaten so far today?"

I glared at Mom, then told Bob everything she'd *made* me eat that morning. Mom had cooked my breakfast, then stood over me while I ate. Watched while I took bite after endless bite and stared until my glass was empty. I'd hated her the whole time.

But right then, with Bob staring at me, I was a teensy bit glad Mom had made me eat. Because I could answer Bob honestly. He'd realize I wasn't sick and he'd send me home!

(He didn't send me home.)

Bob acted like he didn't believe a word coming out of my mouth. I wonder if my parents called ahead to tell him about the Treadmill Incident. The Treadmill Incident definitely needs capital letters. Mom's eyes still shoot laser beams whenever she mentions it. Dad gets that hurt look on his face, where he bites his lip so hard there's a line but he *still* doesn't tell me why he's upset.

Bob made tons of notes in my chart. Then a nurse came in. Her scrubs had squirrels all over them. Or maybe they were chipmunks. I always mix those two up. They're like alligators and crocodiles that way. Or stalagmites and stalactites. Who can remember the difference?

The nurse made me change into one of those faded hospital gowns, the ones five million people have already bled and sweated on. (They *say* they wash them, but who really knows? Maybe there's no laundry detergent budget here and they just dunk them in water.) The gown covered most of me, but I felt like it was see-through, like the nurse was staring at every inch of my skin. Like she was checking to see if I was skinny enough to be in here.

She weighed me with my back to the scale so I couldn't see the number.

She didn't *tell* me the number, either.

I wonder what she *thought* about the number. I wonder if the doctors and nurses are talking about it right now, laughing about my weight in some back room somewhere. Like Talia London did after my BMI test last year.

I hate Talia London.

Talia's at school right now. Talia's going to track practice today, getting ready for the meet on Friday and for regionals next month. Talia's not in a hospital, eating food a bazillion times a day. Talia would never get sent to a hospital for *anything*. Talia's too perfect, with her perfect brown hair and her perfect rosy cheeks and her perfect fingernails that she never, ever bites.

I hate Talia London.

The nurse took my temperature and my blood pressure. Then

she made me stand up so she could do it all over again. I pretended the cuff was a snake wrapping around my arm, cutting off my circulation.

Death by snake would have been better than going through an entire "intake interview," where Mom told Boring Bob every awful thing I've done for the past year and every way I've disappointed her or scared her or made her feel like the WORST. MOM. EVER. She even brought up how she's afraid this is *all her fault*. (With tears in her eyes, of course.)

Which meant I had to comfort Mom so I wouldn't look like an even *worse* daughter in front of Bob. I hate guilt trips like that. And the second I said, "Mom, it's not your fault," Mom's tears cleared up and a relieved smile washed across her face. She didn't consider the possibility that even if this isn't *all* her fault, she might still have done *something* wrong.

Apparently I'm the only criminal around here.

Mom and Dad say that I *should* be in control of my brain. I *should* be able to "turn this craziness off." I should be a lot of things:

Skinny.

Artistic.

Smart.

Athletic.

Julia.

But now I'm stuck here. Bob sent us back to the waiting room with a packet of graham crackers and a juice box, while Squirrel

Nurse and whatever evil committee lives up here on the third floor determined that I'm "medically compromised." Not medically compromised enough to have an IV like Ali, but enough to be stuck inside this prison.

(But how sick is Ali really if she's doing crunches in the middle of the night? Because she *was* doing crunches. There's no other explanation for what I saw.)

"We don't trust you to do this on your own anymore. You need more support than we can give." Mom sounded like she was reading from a script. She definitely wasn't saying the real truth: *You're in here so they can fix you. So I don't have to deal with the less-than-perfect daughter in front of me.*

———

Mom called me selfish last week, when we had that big fight about her putting butter on the green beans behind my back. I thought she was going to throw her plate at me. Either that or stuff the beans down my throat.

"I don't want butter," I said through gritted teeth. I never knew that was an actual thing you could do, but my jaw ached from clenching them so hard.

"You need butter. You're too skinny."

A thrill went through me when Mom said that. A thrill *still* shoots through me every time *anyone* says that. It's the same way

I feel when I step on the scale and see a lower number. It's the thrill of success, the kind I imagine Julia feels when she sticks a landing. The kind I felt last year, when I tried out for the Bay State Blazes and made the team.

"Stop being so selfish," Mom hissed. She turned it into this big thing about how I'm starving for attention (she actually said *starving*) and making myself sick to get back at her for never being around.

(I think Mom's been reading too many articles about eating disorders. And I think *Starving for Attention* was the movie they showed us in health class last year.)

Mom doesn't know what she's talking about. I'm not doing this for revenge and I'm not jealous of her job. I know she needs to make money. I know she likes working and it keeps her "personally fulfilled" or whatever. I'm not even jealous of Julia. I just want to be skinny. Is that so wrong? Mom wants to be skinny, too. I've heard her complain about her thighs and her stomach.

So why is she yelling at me for wanting the same thing?

When Bob came back and told us I was staying, Mom got my suitcase out of the trunk. It used to be Dad's suitcase, actually. The leather is cracked and it's this weird faded shade of brown. There are two buckles on it, and an old luggage tag is tied to the handle: ORLANDO, FLORIDA. I'd way rather be in Orlando right now. I'd way rather be in *Siberia* right now.

I'd rather be in Siberia *naked*.

Mom had packed the suitcase like I was going on a trip. Everything was folded neatly, and she added one of those sachet things so my clothes would smell good. The rose scent made me gag when I opened the suitcase. There are three pairs of sweatpants, two hoodies, three T-shirts, five pairs of underwear, and four pairs of socks. Comfy stuff. Cozy stuff. Baggy stuff. Good. They'll hide the hideousness my body is about to become.

Mom helped me unpack. She put everything into the scratched dresser against the wall. I wonder how clean those drawers are. I bet there are mouse droppings or dead ants in there. Not that it matters. Those clothes are going right back in my suitcase as soon as I convince the therapist or whoever's in charge that I'm not sick.

Mom gave me this journal before she left. It was wrapped in shiny pink paper with a sparkly bow. She beamed as I opened it. "This will be great!" she exclaimed. "You can write about your feelings! It'll help you get better."

I bet that was in one of Mom's articles: HOW JOURNALING CAN CURE YOUR SICK CHILD. I saw her search history the other day when I checked my e-mail on her laptop:

Twelve-year-old daughter + anorexia

Daughter hates me

Ways to add more calories to food

How can parents help + eating disorder

I deleted Mom's search history after I saw it. I wish I'd been able to delete her memory, too. Then she'd believe nothing's wrong.

That I'm "naturally" skinny.

That I'm not *really* sick.

She believed that once, before it got too hard to hide everything. Maybe I can convince everyone else to believe it, too.

———

The girls talk a lot at meals here. They play games, too. They ask one another questions: "What color would you want to dye your hair?" "Have you ever kissed anyone?" Then they giggle until the counselor tells them to concentrate on their food.

Heather's in charge of meals today. She tries to be nice, but I know she's judging me for all the food I had to eat.

I bet she thinks I eat too much.

She'd be right. I'm so full. So disgusting.

I tried to tell Heather I was full, but she didn't believe me.

I bet they won't believe anything I say here. I bet everyone thinks I'm a liar. Mom said that exact thing after the Treadmill Incident.

"I can't believe anything you say anymore. It's like you're a different person."

Duh, I'm a different person. I'm twelve now. Things change when you get to middle school. Mom is definitely *not* my best friend anymore, especially when she does sneaky stuff to fatten me up.

Being skinny doesn't change, though. It's constant. It's safe.

At one point, everyone was talking about the scariest thing they'd ever done. One girl, Laura, talked about how her plane had to do an emergency landing. Another girl, Aisha, talked about giving a speech in front of the whole school. Brenna talked about coming out as bi to her friends.

Ali isn't saying anything. She keeps looking at me, then looking away again, back at her food or at another girl or even at the ceiling. Every time I catch her eye, she presses her lips together. She's not mad, but she's not happy. Is she suspicious? Does she know I saw her last night? Does she hate me?

Everyone's my age, but they seem so much older. They know what's going on around here. They're funny and silly. They talk to one another and have inside jokes. They might be scared of planes and talking in front of crowds, but they don't seem to be falling apart.

I'm already in pieces. I'm scared of my food and not running and gaining weight. I'm scared at home and I'm scared at school. I'm scared of what will happen when I get out of here. I'm scared of having to stay *in* here forever.

When it was my turn, I didn't say anything. I stared at my

plate, at the stack of turkey and lettuce and mayonnaise in front of me. I hate mayonnaise. It looks like milky snot.

This is the scariest thing I've ever done.

———

I'm sick of writing, but there's nothing else to do during this free time. So I'm keeping my head down and my hands busy. That way, no one will come over and talk about the Red Sox or climate change or how *awesome* it is that I'm here. I'm writing and trying to draw the television across the room. That's the kind of picture Mom displays in her gallery, paintings of fax machines and printers done by fancy-schmancy artists wearing horn-rimmed glasses and skinny jeans. Artists who talk about stuff like "the dangers of technology" and how "the color gray symbolizes the downfall of society."

Drawing electronics isn't *fun*, though. Plus, I'm still awful at that whole "perspective" thing Mom tried to teach me. The window behind the TV looks too small.

This is exactly why I took a drawing break. Because nothing I draw is good enough.

I keep getting distracted, too. I don't think my stomach is working right. Aren't stomachs supposed to digest food? The food is sitting like a boulder in mine. Like a mountain. Mount Fuji is in my stomach.

Don't think about it. Don't think about it. Think about anything but food. Think about the walls. They're pink. Salmon pink.

Salmon is food.

This is not working.

I didn't know where to sit for group, so I sat in a blue armchair. I feel like it's my first day at a new school and I have no friends.

I feel like I did that day in the lunchroom, when Talia convinced everyone they shouldn't sit with me because of my tuna fish sandwich. When the other kids held their noses when I walked by and sniffed around me before they sat down in class.

When they called me Rancid Riley. Roly-Poly Riley.

I'm not that girl anymore, though. I never will be again.

There are five other girls here besides Ali: Brenna, Meredith, Laura, Rebecca, and Aisha. That's a lot of new people to keep track of, so I'm keeping a cheat sheet in here, even though I won't be tested on this. (I hope.)

Brenna is sitting next to me. She's white, kind of big, and has brown hair, a pixie cut, and bright yellow sneakers. She's wearing the coolest outfit, too: an orange Camp Half-Blood T-shirt, a pair of blue Ravenclaw socks, *and* a *My Little Pony* button. (Emerson says we're too old for *My Little Pony*, but she's totally wrong. There's no age limit on sparkle.)

Aisha is short and skinny. She's black, with super-short, curly hair and glasses. Her shirt is this bright turquoise color with pink and orange threads woven all through it that makes her look like a human rainbow. A smiley rainbow.

Meredith is on the couch across from me. Meredith is black, too, with long hair and pretty brown eyes. She's also sitting up so straight my back hurts just looking at her. That's because Meredith is a ballerina. It's totally obvious, and not just because of the ballet slippers on her shirt. Meredith's skin is pimple-free and her hair is in a bun. Ballerina is a costume she can never slip out of.

Laura's sitting next to me. She's white, with these really piercing blue eyes. Her long blond hair is perfectly straight and her cheeks are bright, like she just put on blush. We're not allowed to wear makeup in here, though, so maybe she's just naturally rosy. The rest of her isn't rosy, though. Laura's eyes are narrowed and her bottom lip is stuck out. If she was a dwarf, she'd be Scary. Or maybe Skinny. I wonder if I'm that skinny.

I hope I'm not.

I kind of hope I am.

Laura keeps trying to look at what I'm writing, which is why my handwriting is super jerky. I have to keep shifting and angling my body. I stopped myself from giving her a dirty look, because the last thing I want is an enemy in here. (*Another* one, I mean.)

Rebecca's hiding in her sweatshirt, her head swallowed by the hood like a turtle withdrawing into its shell. All I can see are her pale, freckled cheeks and the outline of an athlete's body. She looks strong. Muscular. Dad used to call me strong. That was back when I was fat, though, before I started running.

Ali and Aisha are laughing about something they saw on TV last night. That's what everyone does at night here. After visiting hours, we can watch TV or movies or read or play board games. No internet. No magazines. Just talking and "appropriate" media. We can also go to our rooms. That's what I did last night. Now I feel left out, though.

Ali laughs a lot. She doesn't seem to notice her IV much, either. She's waving her arms around and making funny faces. (I think Ali actually has *more* freckles than Rebecca.) Maybe she's used to the IV. She said she's been here a week already. I doubt a week will be enough for me to feel comfortable with *anything* here.

Ali's still super skinny, too. Is that because she's doing all those crunches? Will I stay skinny if I do crunches, too? But what if they catch me and keep me here even longer?

I don't think Ali's worried about that, though. Right now, she's swishing her long brown hair around and laughing, even though there's nothing funny about this place at all.

———

Assertiveness Group was boring. We talked about . . . wait for it . . . ways we can be more assertive in real life. Are you shocked? I know I am.

We got homework, too. Booooo.

Now it's free time. I'm supposed to meet with my therapist, but not for another fifteen minutes. The other girls have appointments, too. Or they're doing art projects. Or talking. Or in their rooms napping. People are big on naps here.

I don't want to do any of that. I don't want to have fun or make something cute or find a new friend. I want to pout like a little kid.

———

It happened last year, halfway through sixth grade. I was sitting in homeroom when everything started. Mr. Lin passed out a handout, like the teachers always do at the beginning of the day. I usually stuff them in my backpack until Mom fishes them out and yells at me for being disorganized.

I couldn't forget about this one, though:

Dear Parents,
This letter is to inform you of the Body Mass Index (BMI)
Screening Program that will be happening soon at Hawthorne
Middle School. In compliance with the state of Massachusetts's
BMI reporting and recording requirements, the Body Mass Index
of all sixth graders will be calculated on Thursday of next week.

Students will be called down to the nurse's office by class on
their assigned day, and your child's privacy will be respected at all
times. After results are calculated, our health staff will follow up
with your child's weight status and give recommendations so your
child can have the best and healthiest school year possible.

Please indicate whether or not you give permission and return this form to your child's teacher by Friday.

Sincerely,
Katherine Hunt, Principal

I didn't think Mom would give permission. Mom hates weighing herself in front of other people, so why would she let me do it? Just in case, though, I threw the form away.

Of course, Principal Hunt e-mailed the information to all our parents. So when I got home from school that afternoon, the printed-out and signed permission slip was waiting on the kitchen counter.

Miranda Logan <u>DOES</u> give permission for Riley to participate in BMI testing.

Mom told me it was important to learn healthy habits early. That I'd been eating too many Brown Sugar Cinnamon Pop-Tarts and not enough vegetables. She even asked Julia's coach for the Proper Nutrition handout she gives to the older kids.

I should have told Mom that I could eat whatever I wanted, that Brown Sugar Cinnamon Pop-Tarts were a present to the world with frosting on top. I should have told her that I wasn't a gymnast and that my body was different from Julia's. I should have "lost" the permission slip. Asked for a new one and forged her name.

Because then Talia wouldn't have heard the number.

No one was supposed to hear my number. They even mentioned "privacy" in the letter. Nurse Shaw closed her door between each student as we stood in a line outside her office.

Talia was behind me. She's always behind me. Riley Logan. Talia London. I can never get away from her perfect hair and perfect skin and perfect cheekbones. I wish Nurse Shaw was perfect. Then she wouldn't have left the door open a crack while I was in there. She wouldn't have spoken so loudly after I got off the scale.

"Overweight." She said it like she was a judge sentencing me to death. In sixth grade, being big *is* worse than death.

No, being big and having the snottiest girl in school find out is worse than death.

"Riley's overweight!" Talia started laughing. Behind her, Camille did, too.

I wanted to rip the calculator out of Nurse Shaw's hands.

I wanted to smash *her* scale on the floor.

I wanted to disappear.

Of course Talia was laughing. *She* didn't eat stuff like Pop-Tarts and mayonnaise. She never ate cupcakes during class parties. When we were in fifth grade, she was the first kid to wear a bikini.

At lunch that day, Talia stared at my pizza slice like it was a bomb about to explode on my thighs. She giggled with her friends. I knew they were talking about me.

I ate my pizza that day because I was hungry. But I didn't eat my dessert. I kept hearing the word *overweight*. I kept seeing the scale.

Talia kept teasing me, too. Not all the time, but enough so that I never forgot I was overweight. She laughed at my lunch, even when I started bringing a salad like her. Even when I started bringing nothing.

I should have told her to be quiet. I should have told her that my weight was none of her business. I should have told her lots of things. I didn't, though. I didn't want Talia to make fun of me any more than she already did.

Emerson and Josie told me to ignore her, but Talia was already in my head. I kept bringing salads to school. I kept bringing nothing.

The number on the scale started going down.

Lower.

Lower.

Lower.

I started running more.

Longer.

Longer.

Longer.

I wasn't overweight anymore. The numbers told me that.

But I didn't listen.

———

My therapist's name is Willow. Of course. I *knew* she was going to be all earthy-crunchy. I bet her middle name is Dandelion. Or Moonfairy. I bet she has long hair and a crown of flowers, that she wears tie-dyed shirts and long beaded skirts.

I bet Willow will try to analyze my dreams to "uncover the great trauma in my past." But what if she tries to hypnotize me and discovers that my big trauma is nothing more than a few silly comments made by a silly girl in my class? Shouldn't I have been strong enough to not let that break me? Shouldn't there be a bigger *reason* that I'm like this? Because if there isn't, then why *am* I like this? Why am I sick and Julia isn't?

I should make up something to tell Willow. I'll say something about how Mom always tells me I'm fat and that's why I don't eat. Chloe's mom is like that. That's why Mrs. Fitzgerald makes her run track: so she can lose weight. Chloe hates track, too. She complains about it all the time and says she has her period like three times a month.

I don't know if I could keep track of a big lie, though. And part of me actually *wants* to be honest with Willow. Part of me is tired of lying. Part of me is sad that my best friend *and* my mom hate me. Maybe Willow can help me. Maybe life without starving and running and worrying *is* possible.

As long as I don't get *really* huge.

I checked my e-mail before my appointment with Willow. There's a shared computer in the hallway we can sign up for during afternoon free time. Ten-minute sessions, no extensions. Brenna was looking at some book blog, but she let me use her last five minutes.

All I had was an e-mail from Principal Hunt saying corny stuff like "We believe in you!" and "The staff is excited to have you back and healthy again!" She'd added five smiley faces at the end.

I guess that's the one good thing about being in here: I get a break from schoolwork. Not that I've been learning much at school. I've barely been able to concentrate the past few months. That was Mom and Dad's first clue: my Bs dropped to Cs. I went from an above-average to an average student.

And for Mom and Dad, average sets off alarm bells.

I'm hearing alarm bells now, too. Because I didn't have *any* mail from my friends. There was nothing from Josie. Nothing even from Emerson. I wish I could text them, but that's against the rules. They took my phone away the second I walked through the unit door, like it was covered in contaminated slime. Jean said they want to "remove technology's hold on me," to "separate me from the world of my disease." I feel like they've cut off a limb.

I'd almost *rather* they cut off one of my fingers. I could survive without a pinkie. Maybe even a thumb, although that might make things tricky. It'd be hard to hold a marker to draw. It'd even be hard to do something simple, like opening up a plastic baggie. But I could give up plastic baggies if it meant being able to text with Emerson and Josie.

If they'd even text back.

There are no crystals in Willow's office. No rainbows or moonbeams, either. She seems normal, actually, which is annoying. I want there to be something to hate about her, a reason to be rude and stick my tongue out at her. A reason to *not* talk, even though part of me is dying to let everything out.

Willow's nice, at least. She's thin, but the *healthy* kind of thin. The kind with muscles on her arms and thighs and a little pouch on her stomach. She wears normal clothes: jeans and a plain blue button-down shirt. Her curly blond hair is half falling out of her ponytail. She's pretty, but not so pretty that I'm jealous. When Willow smiles, her eyes crinkle at the edges.

That's how you know someone's giving you a real smile, that they're not a faking faker like Talia London. Talia fakes nice all the time. The corners of her mouth turn up, but her eyes are ice-cold. She fake sneezes, too, then wrinkles her nose and tries to look all cute. Like a sneeze could ever be cute.

Jacob Sullivan thinks so, though. That's probably why he asked Talia to be his girlfriend. Either that or because she's way prettier than me. Skinnier than me, too. I bet she wears a size 0000000. If that was a size, I bet Talia would wear it.

I hate Talia. I hate her sneeze and her smile and her laugh. I even hate her teeth. They're too white. Teeth should *not* be that white and perfect.

I told Willow about Talia. I don't know how it happened. I was trying so hard not to talk about food that when she asked me what was on my mind, I blurted it out really fast: "I hate Talia London."

Then I clamped my mouth shut. Why did I say anything? Now Willow won't think I'm fine. She won't think I'm perfect.

At least Willow didn't lecture me like Mom would have, about how hate isn't a nice way to feel and how I should always choose kindness. Instead, Willow said that it's totally normal to not like people. That even *she* hates people.

That was nice of her.

Except then Willow babbled on about how important it is to feel my emotions and not stuff them down. She gave me a handout with twenty cartoon faces on it, each labeled with an emotion:

Guilty.

Sad.

Anxious.

Ecstatic.

Scared.

Frustrated.

Cautious.

"What's your emotion right now?" Willow asked.

All of the above? None of the above? Sometimes I don't know whether I feel too much or nothing at all. I closed my eyes and waved my hand over the handout, like I used to do with Julia when we played the "Where Are You Going on Vacation?" game.

We'd drag Dad's dusty old globe off the bookshelf in his office, close our eyes, and spin the world around. Wherever our finger landed was where we'd supposedly be going on vacation that year.

France. Kazakhstan. Easter Island. Mozambique.

It was fun to imagine an exotic trip, especially when most of our vacations are tacked on to Julia's gymnastics meets all over New England. We stay in a hotel room on the same floor as the rest of her teammates. I sit in a stuffy gym for hours, then pretend to be excited about dinner at a chain restaurant and the hotel pool.

An imaginary vacation to France would be way better than all of that.

I could tell that Willow was stifling a sigh when my finger wiggled in the air and then landed on *jealous*. I bet she's already sick of me. Mom and Dad shipped me off, and now Ms. Therapist Who's Supposed to Change My Life is ready to kick me out of her office. No wonder Talia made fun of me. No wonder Josie hates me. I'm toxic.

Willow didn't kick me out, though. Probably because she's a professional. She folded her hands on her lap and pretended everything was normal. "Who are you jealous of?"

My mind flashed to Julia, to the looks of pride on Mom and Dad's faces when she sticks a tricky vault. To the finish line at the track, which I never, ever cross first. To Ali's body crunching up and down.

"No one. Never mind."

During snack today, Aisha asked me if I'd been in treatment before. She asked me like it was a totally normal question, like she was asking me what my favorite TV show was.

"Um . . . no? Have you?"

"Oh yeah. This is my fourth time here."

Four times? Once is enough for me. Once is too *many* times for me. Why does Aisha keep coming back? Does that mean treatment doesn't work? I thought I was supposed to come in here and be cured. (I'm not sure if I *want* to be cured, but they should at least have truth in advertising or whatever.)

If Aisha keeps coming back, what if I have to come back, too? What if I decide I want to recover and try really hard and am honest with Willow? What if I trust the staff and gain weight and then have to come back and go through this awfulness *all over again*?

What if this place is like one of those fancy revolving doors in front of hotels, the ones that go around and around? What if I get stuck in that loop forever?

No. I have to get out of here now. Get out and get a little bit better. Enough so nobody notices the sick parts of me anymore. Enough so I feel better.

In our appointment, Willow told me that to get rid of my eating disorder, I have to "make the decision to get better." I have to

42

decide that health and happiness and not being weak and hungry all the time is better than the number on the scale.

Maybe Aisha hasn't decided yet and that's why she's back.

I understand *that*. I can't believe people when they say that recovery is a good thing. Because I don't want a *good* thing. I want a *sure* thing. I want them to tell me they can cure me. That if I eat this food and follow this meal plan and am the perfect patient, *then* I'll be happy.

I'd recover if I could get that guarantee. The guarantee that when I leave, no one will make fun of me. That Mom will be proud of me. That Dad will notice me. That my friends will like me no matter how much I mess up.

No one can do that, though. They can't guarantee anything.

So I'll stick with the sure thing, even though it hurts sometimes. Even though (late at night, when my stomach aches and I'm filled with regret instead of food) sometimes I wish I'd never started losing weight in the first place.

I *did* start, though. And now I'm not Roly-Poly Riley anymore. I'm Runner Riley. Skinny Riley.

I don't have to get stuck in that revolving door. I'm stronger than Aisha. I'll get a little better, but not *too much* better. I'll fool them all.

And when I leave, I *won't* come back.

—

Dinner. Meal four. I'm going to stop counting the times I eat here. I don't think I can count that high.

There's a cutout of Elsa on the wall of the dining room. LET IT GO is spelled out on top, in alternating dark blue and light blue construction-paper letters. Taped around Elsa are white snowflakes that patients wrote on. Past patients, I bet, because I didn't recognize any of the names:

I let go of my desire to be perfect. —Carah

I let go of my routines. —Anna

I let go of the eating disorder's insults. —Ivy

Lots of the snowflakes are filled, but there are still a bunch of empty ones. I'm not ready to fill one out yet. Thinking about letting go of my eating disorder is scary. It's good and bad all rolled up together, like the scarves Mom makes with two different-colored balls of yarn. When she knits her stitches together so tightly, you can't separate one color from the other.

My mind feels like that now. There's too much going on. I don't want to change, but I *do* want to turn my brain off. I want my head to be quieter. I want to be happier.

Brenna sat next to me at dinner. She started humming some song I kind of recognized, by that band Josie was obsessed with last year. *Doo-doo-DOOOOO. Dum-DUM-DUM-dahhhhh.*

I let Brenna distract me. *All* the girls distracted me. Or maybe we distracted one another. We talked about school dances and how silly they are. Ali told us how her mom chaperoned her last dance and actually walked over and *fixed her hair*. I'd totally die.

Laura told us how her boyfriend, Timothy, brought her lilacs before their first dance as boyfriend and girlfriend, but that she's allergic to lilacs. "My eyes started watering so much that I looked like I was crying." Laura giggled. It's the first time I've seen her giggle since I've been here.

Brenna said one of her teachers yelled at her for wearing pants to the Christmas Dance, but that the girl she likes danced with her.

Meredith said she'd never been to a school dance, because she always has ballet practice on Friday nights. "*Had* practice, I mean." She looked sad and poked at her pasta until the counselor told her to watch her "behaviors." That's what the staff calls practically everything we do here. If we eat too fast or too slowly, it's an eating disorder "behavior." If we chew too many times, it's a behavior. If we *look* at our food the wrong way, it's a behavior.

I had to turn my attention back to my food mountain then, the one I have to climb six times a day. Each step I take, it gets steeper and steeper.

Brenna must have been able to tell I was freaked, because she nudged my shoulder. "It's hard, but you can do it," she said. "It gets easier. Take it one bite at a time and I'll distract you." Brenna started talking about this awesome comic she's reading, *Ms. Marvel*. I'm not really into comics, but it sounded really cool. Female superheroes! Girls who aren't just sidekicks!

"I cosplay as Ms. Marvel, too," Brenna said. Then she blushed. "I can't believe I told you that. It's so embarrassing."

"No, it's cool," I said. "I'd love to pretend to be someone else for a while, too."

I took a deep breath and told Brenna about the drawings I used to do, about the unicorns and castles and dragons. About the fancy stuff Mom wanted me to draw instead, because I have "so much talent."

I talked instead of eating. Brenna ate while I talked.

"Slow down, Brenna," the counselor said. "Remember to chew and enjoy the food."

Brenna blushed. She took a sip of her milk. She avoided my eyes.

I wonder if Brenna has bulimia. Or binge-eating disorder. She *is* bigger than me, after all. I wonder if she's trying to *stop* herself from eating as much as I'm trying to make myself *start*. I wonder if her blush means she's embarrassed.

Should she be embarrassed?

Before I got in here, I probably would have said yes. I would have said that eating too much is gross. That being big is gross. But Brenna is cool. I like to talk to her. I don't care that she's bigger than me. I don't care what she looks like.

Maybe people don't care what I look like, either.

I didn't say any of that out loud, though. I told her that I'm not drawing much anymore, and that all my stuff is at home, in sketchbooks shoved in the back of my closet. I didn't tell her about the stuff I've been working on in here. No one wants to see my awful drawing of a television.

"I'd like to see them someday." Brenna smiled. "I bet you're way better than me."

I bet I'm not.

At least talking to Brenna helped me get through dinner. I forgot (mostly) about the food in front of me. I forgot about the bites I took.

Then it was over. The counselor rang a little bell and we left the dining room.

Another meal conquered.

On to the next one.

Brenna may be cool and Willow may listen to me, but I hate feeling so gross after a meal. There's a 99 percent chance my stomach is going to explode.

99.9 percent, even.

They'll have to let me go home then, right?

I can't do this for another day.

I can't do this for the rest of my life.

The staff may say recovery's a good thing, but they have to be lying. This treatment thing is a big scam, a way to get our insurance companies to pay them zillions of dollars.

Why did I think for one second that I maybe wanted to recover? My body is falling apart.

I'll eat as long as I'm here, but I'm stopping the second I get home.

———

I called Mom tonight to tell her about my day. About the counting-while-I-pee thing. About how much I'm eating. About how Brenna's not so bad and Willow's kind of nice. I didn't say anything about Ali and her crunches, though. I like the idea of keeping that secret to myself for a bit. Like how Dad always sticks a granola bar in his backpack for later.

Just in case he needs it.

I asked Mom to tell Emerson and Josie to e-mail me. I asked her to visit, to bring books and my special markers, the ones I stuffed in my bottom desk drawer when running started taking over my life. At first, I didn't mention the markers. I was afraid Mom would start talking about my "potential" and gushing that I "shouldn't have stopped; you were definitely going places."

I think Mom's scared to admit the truth: that I'm not going places.

I'm not going anywhere.

I'll never display my silly animals or faces in Mom's gallery.

I'll never win an award for my art.

And now that I'm in the hospital, I'll never be the skinniest.

I still asked for my markers, though. They're nothing fancy, but they do have two sides, one thick tip and one super-thin one, so I can work on details. I have one hundred colors, too. (Well, ninety-eight now. I somehow lost lime green and rose pink.)

Mom agreed to bring them without a word about my "lost future as an artist."

That's *one* good thing about today.

DAY THREE: WEDNESDAY

There was a part of me that thought I'd wake up this morning different. That one full day of treatment would change me and I'd be recovered already. That I'd want to change.

I'd wake up and stretch in a beam of sunlight, then bound out of bed and eat a huge breakfast. Pancakes and syrup and bacon and eggs. I wouldn't count calories and I wouldn't feel my stomach for flab. I wouldn't run my fingers up and down my sides, making sure nothing had changed. I wouldn't want to go for a run.

I wouldn't wake up powered by a motor I don't know how to stop.

I believed all that until I actually *did* wake up. And my brain proved it's just as broken as ever.

I wanted to bound out of bed, but not to eat breakfast. I wanted to go for a run.

I ran my fingers up and down my sides.

I felt my hips, my chest, and my cheekbones.

I cried.

I'm still here.

I'm not different.

I never will be.

———

I haven't told Mom the truth. I haven't told anyone the truth. I don't want to. If I reveal my deepest secret, someone will grab on to it and never let go. They'll use it as proof that I *want* to get better. That I want to gain weight.

Ali understands, though. We talked about it last night, after the night nurse, Nicole, had turned off our lights, when the only illumination was the glow of the nurses' station down the hall, the only other sounds the soft whispers of the staff patrolling the halls.

"It's scary to think about recovery," I whispered. Ali had been quiet for a while, but I could tell she was awake. Julia and I used to share a room, so I'm an expert at stuff like that. When you're asleep, your breathing is even and steady. There are fewer pauses and fewer sniffles. Ali wasn't sniffling, but her sheets were rustling. They're thin and scratchy and almost as loud as the wind outside. She rolled over to face me, so I kept talking. "It's scary to think about trusting everyone here. They tell me that life will be better without an eating disorder, that my body won't hurt anymore and I won't be sad. But—"

"What if it's not?"

I nodded, even though Ali probably couldn't see me.

Heather said during group yesterday that once I gain weight, my brain will work better. It will be easier to stop obsessing about food and I'll be happier. I want to believe her. I really do.

Because *that's* my deepest, darkest secret: I hate being like this. It makes me sad and it makes me hungry and it makes me hurt. I say that I like being skinny, that I like not eating, but that's not true all the time.

I want to be like Emerson, who eats two peanut butter sandwiches before track practice and a bag of M&M's after.

I want to be like Josie, who has time to do other stuff, like computer club and Girl Scouts, because she doesn't have to run all the time.

They go to parties and sleepovers. *They* have full stomachs so they can fall asleep at night.

That's why I didn't fight so hard when Mom told me they were sending me here. That someone else would make me eat. Because I *do* want to be like everyone else. Deep down inside, I want to be like them so, so badly. I want to not run every day. I want to draw again and not worry what Mom or anyone else will say. I want to eat my birthday cake. I want to be normal.

But at the same time . . . I don't.

Because then I wouldn't be skinny. Why is skinny so important to me? How can I *know* I want other things and then keep getting stuck on skinny? It's like a bad song I can't get out of my head. I want to turn the music off, but I can't.

Maybe Ali feels the same way. Maybe she's here because she "kind of" wants to get better. Maybe she's doing crunches because she also "kind of" wants to stay sick.

Maybe Ali has the right idea.

Maybe I should stay sick, too.

Because if I'm not skinny, who will I be?

———

I was the last one to the weigh-in room this morning, because I had to go to the bathroom. I had to count again, too. I made it to fifty-two before my body relaxed enough to pee.

All the other girls were in a row when I got there. Brenna. Meredith. Ali. Laura. Aisha. Rebecca. I got behind Rebecca and stared at the floor: no dirt, no streaks, not even a scuff mark. I wonder when the janitor comes in. Maybe they make *us* clean the floor. We'll have to get down there with toothbrushes and scrub until it's spotless. Like little Cinderellas. (Except cleaning burns calories, so there's no way that'd happen.)

One at a time, the other girls went into the room next to the nurses' station. I imagined it to be all stainless steel and glass tables. Super high-tech, like on that doctors-as-spies show Josie's obsessed with but I think is totally ridiculous. (Who has time to be a doctor *and* a spy? When would they get any sleep?) It was a normal room, though, like the pediatrician's, except without the basket of stickers on the counter.

But all I saw was the scale.

Nicole took my vitals first. She did it while I was sitting and then while I was standing, like Squirrel Scrubs did when I got here. I guess whatever numbers she got were bad, because she made me drink a cup of orange Gatorade. The people here act like Gatorade is some sort of magical potion.

Drinking from that plastic cup made me feel like I was at a track meet. Like the one I'll be missing this week, where everyone will be drinking Gatorade without me. Doing the pre-meet cheer without me. Burning calories without me.

Living life without me.

I miss laughing with Emerson while we wait for our heats. I miss making fun of silly action movies with Josie. I miss being normal, instead of a stuck-in-a-hospital freak.

When Nicole finally weighed me, she made me step onto the scale backward again. Apparently that's the way *everyone* does it here. I don't get to know my weight.

Which is *so* not fair. It's my weight, not Nicole's. But when I tried to argue with her, she pointed to the scale in that "I know best and you don't because you're a kid" way. I hate when grown-ups do that.

The scale was different from Mom's at home. Mom's is a bright pink Weight Watchers scale she bought at Walmart. This one is top-of-the-line. It's silver and sleek and see-through.

I don't trust it. Just like I shouldn't have trusted Nurse Shaw.

What if Nicole tells everyone my weight like Nurse Shaw did? What if everyone laughs at how huge I am?

When Nicole wrote in my file, I tried to see how her hand was moving. Was that a two? A five? I couldn't tell.

"Can you *please* tell me?" I begged. "It's my first week." I forced a waver into my voice. That's how I get Grandma and Grandpa Logan to let me watch extra TV when we visit them.

Nicole didn't say a word. Ali told me she was strict.

I want to sneak into the locked office and read my file. The number is in there: on a piece of paper, in a folder, in a drawer, in a file cabinet somewhere. It's out in the world, judging me.

How am I supposed to know what to do if I don't know what I weigh?

———

In group this morning, Heather said that people with eating disorders are our own worst critics. That means we obsess over our flaws and make them a bigger deal than they really are.

So it's not like how Julia gets stressed out when she takes the teensiest step forward on her uneven bars landing.

How Emerson hates the mole on her cheek.

How Josie is self-conscious because her big toes are super short.

For us, it's worse.

"The difference is that you guys can focus on those flaws *too much*," Heather says. "They transform into something so big that they start to define you."

"Like the Incredible Hulk!" Brenna shouted out. "First he's this calm scientist guy, Bruce Banner, but when he gets all anxious, he turns into a huge green muscly dude." She pounded her fists on her hoodie.

Am I like the Incredible Hulk, too? What's my flaw?

My body, obviously. I'm not small enough. I'm not fast enough, either.

Plus, I'm not a good artist.

That's not just my opinion, either. It's a fact. We learned about facts in science class. A fact is something you can prove, something that can be backed up by evidence.

My evidence that I'm not a good artist is that I didn't make the school art show last year. I worked really hard on my drawing, too. First I was going to draw the monument on the town common. Mom loves stuff like that. Drawing statues is boring, though, and it kept raining every time I sat out with my sketch pad.

Then I decided to draw a mermaid. I'm awesome at mermaids. But that was boring, too. (Probably because I've drawn seven billion trillion of them already.)

So I challenged myself. I tried something different and did a self-portrait. I drew and redrew it until it was perfect. I shaded and shadowed and colored until even the nose looked right. Then I submitted it to the school art show. I *knew* I was going to get in. Maybe I'd even be the featured display. That's the piece they prop up on the table in front of the door, the one under the banner that says WELCOME, FUTURE ARTISTS!

Mom and Dad would go to the show and exclaim over my drawing. They would brag that *their* daughter was the superstar of the show. Talia would apologize for always being so mean.

But I wasn't the featured display.

I didn't even make it into the show.

That's why I have to be my worst critic.

I have to beat everyone else to it.

———

I tried to call Mom before breakfast, but she didn't answer. Then I realized she's at work. Julia's at school. The rest of the world hasn't stopped because I'm in here. People are going on with their lives without me. Right now, Emerson's in Language Arts. Josie's in gym, where I should be, too.

Usually, Josie and I laugh and talk through gym class. So much that Mrs. Klick always yells at us. We haven't been laughing lately, though. Josie's too mad at me for skipping her birthday party. I wonder if she'll ever forgive me. Because I didn't mean to hurt her. She doesn't understand.

No one understands.

"You care about your stupid diet more than you care about me! I thought we were best friends!"

We *are* best friends. And this isn't a diet. People can *stop* diets. They stop when they're hungry, before their stomach twists and their head becomes as light as a balloon. I can't stop, though. Sometimes I think I might want to. Sometimes before I go to bed, I tell myself I'll eat more the next day. That I don't *want* to feel so sick anymore. That I don't want to hurt.

Then I wake up and do the same stuff all over again.

If I don't, I'll fall apart.

———

We have a half hour to eat breakfast. A half hour to eat an entire feast. A Thanksgiving Day–worthy feast.

I can't believe I ate it all.

A bunch of the other girls complained that they were full, too. "We just ate dinner, like, five minutes ago." Ali said it quietly, so the counselor couldn't hear.

"Seriously. My stomach should have its own zip code." That was Aisha. Rebecca was the only one who didn't complain, but she never says much outside of group. She's on a different meal plan than most of us, too. She eats less, which made me jealous at first, but I can tell it's still hard for her.

She's bigger than most of us, but not huge. Brenna's the biggest. Not that that's a bad thing. (Is it mean that I wrote that about her? Is it mean that I notice Brenna's body? *Am* I judging her?)

In our Relaxation Group last night, Rebecca said that bingeing makes her feel way better than deep breathing. Then she cringed, like we were all going to make fun of her. I would never laugh at Rebecca, though. Because part of me understands what she meant. Food *is* relaxing. Counting calories makes me forget, like someone stuck me in an isolation chamber and left my problems outside the door.

Maybe eating a lot of food is like that, too.

"This place is a joke." Laura flipped her hair over her shoulder. As usual, Laura's hair is straight and non-frizzy and perfect, like she smuggled a blow-dryer in here. An illegal blow-dryer.

They don't let us have a lot of things on the unit: Electronics. Scissors. Knitting needles (people have to sign them out from the nurses' station). Food, so people don't binge and purge or fill up on something not in their meal plan. There's no food allowed anywhere except the dining room. But there's a *lot* of food there.

I ate everything again. I didn't want to, but I did. If we don't finish our meal in thirty minutes, we have to have a Boost drink. Those things are disgusting. Great-Grandma Logan drank Boosts all the time before she died, after she lost all her teeth and couldn't chew. She gave me a sip once. It tasted like someone mixed up chalk, oatmeal, and strawberries in a blender.

Mom said they're good for old people because they have all the calories of a full meal, but what was good for Great-Grandma is a punishment worse than death (probably not an exaggeration) here. Even if you eat everything except for *one bite*, you *still* have to have a Boost. That's basically like eating *two whole meals* at the same time.

I hope everyone doesn't think I'm gross because I ate everything. Part of me wanted to rebel and throw my food on the floor, but part of me was hungry. Not too hungry, though. Just a little bit. That little bit still freaks me out, though. I shouldn't be hungry. I'm already eating too much.

I wonder if I should have left some of my meal on my plate. Or yelled at a nurse or something. Isn't that what sick people are supposed to do?

They may have told me the official rules here, but no one told me the unofficial ones. The ones girls with eating disorders know by heart. The ones we absorb at the same time we reject or inhale food. The ones that say that competition is normal and that the skinniest girl is queen.

The ones I disobeyed by eating my meal so quickly.

For eating my meal at all.

Ali asked me if she's as skinny as Laura.

"I'm not sure." I *think* Ali is skinnier, but I can't tell for sure. The dress code here is super strict. Stricter than if I went to one of those Catholic schools with the plaid uniforms. Because even if they have to wear collared shirts and sweaters, they can still wear skirts.

Skirts aren't allowed here. Tank tops or shorts, either. We can't expose our legs or our shoulders. Apparently the dress code is so we don't compare our bodies with everyone else's. Like an extra layer of fabric is going to help with that. I started comparing the second I walked in the door. I've been comparing my entire life.

My cousin Ava has an awesome voice. Grandma says she "sings like an angel." I sing like a strangled frog.

Julia's Julia. She's the "great hope" of our town, cooed over since she started doing cartwheels at age two and a half. Julia's future is full of ribbons and trophies, sparkly leotards and cheering crowds. Mine is full of B (now C) grades, fourth-place finishes, and a guarantee that no boy will ever like me.

Mom and Dad tell me they don't love either of us more. But Julia has more ribbons than dust mites in her room. Julia wins everything.

Or she did until two months ago. Two months ago, I looked

at us side by side in the mirror. I saw my brown hair and green eyes, her blond hair and green eyes. I saw my freckles and her mole, our pierced ears.

I saw that I was skinnier than Julia. For once in my life, I, Roly-Poly Riley, was skinnier than Julia the Gymnast.

I'd finally won. I was Runner Riley. Skinny Riley.

I had to stay that way.

So I get why Ali was looking for reassurance. She wanted to know that *she* was still the best at something. To feel that small bit of relief before she starts comparing again.

We *always* start comparing again.

I told her she was definitely skinnier than Laura. I made my voice all confident and self-assured, like Coach Jackson sounds during a track meet.

Great form! Give it a kick! You can do this!

I told Ali her legs look like twigs.

I told Ali her arms look like matchsticks.

I told Ali she looks skinnier than she did when I got here.

I told her everything *I'd* want to hear. Then I asked her how *I* looked. I held my breath while I waited for the answer. I felt like I was on trial and Ali was delivering the verdict.

"You're as skinny as ever."

Not guilty.

———

The one good thing about seeing a therapist is that I'm allowed to complain about stuff. There's no Dad telling me to "Look on the bright side!" or Mom sighing that she doesn't have time for my nonsense. Willow said to tell her about my problems.

So I am.

I told her how my meeting with Caroline the nutritionist was the most boring thing ever. That she told me about food groups like I was in school, then demonstrated with a bunch of measuring cups and plastic play food like I used to have in my toy kitchen when I was a kid.

"Caroline said I'm on the weight-gain meal plan!" I widened my eyes and stuck out my lower lip. I needed to look as sad as possible so Willow would talk to Caroline. So she'd help me get my meal plan changed.

"Of course you are, Riley." Willow arched her eyebrow. "You're in the hospital to gain weight."

"Only a little bit of weight, though." (I think I was whining.)

"No, not a *little bit*."

"Then how much?" (I was *totally* whining.)

"As much as we decide is necessary."

"But I'm fine the way I am! Lots of kids at school are this skinny."

"It doesn't matter what *everyone else* looks like, it matters what *you* look like." Then Willow corrected herself. "Actually, it *doesn't* matter what you look like. It matters that you're healthy."

"I *am* healthy!"

Willow steepled her fingers together. Under her top lip, her tongue ran along her teeth. I wonder if she got anything stuck there during her lunch. I wonder what Willow ate for lunch. I bet her meals are perfectly balanced, but always with a treat at the end. A piece of candy, maybe, or a cookie. I wonder if adults give each other judgy looks when *they* eat cookies.

I wonder what it would be like to eat a cookie and not hate myself. To never be starving between "meals" or worry about how to hide food. That would be nice.

Skinny would be nicer, though.

Willow does these long-silence things a lot. She says she does it to make me think.

It works, too.

"I've been eating all my food," I said finally. "Doesn't that mean I can go home now? That I'm all better?" But even as I asked Willow, I knew she'd say no.

She did. "It's a nice thought, Riley, and I'm glad you're working so hard. But we still have more work to do."

"*I have to go home.*" I articulated every word, like I was an actress trying out for a play. This was my line. Now it was Willow's turn to speak, to tell me that of course I'm better! Of course I have permission to leave and do whatever I want now.

Willow *didn't* remember her lines, though. "Why do you 'have to go home'?" More finger steepling. Willow's fingers are really long, and she has a sparkly ruby ring on her left hand. On her ring finger, too. I wondered if that means she's married, even though it's not a diamond.

So I asked her. "Are you married?"

"We're here to talk about you, not me," Willow said.

Arggh! Willow is super annoying. I take back what I said about her being nice.

"But what if I *want* to talk about you?"

"Then we can do that outside of session," Willow said. "As long as it's appropriate." She babbled something about therapist-patient boundaries or whatever. Like boundaries are so important when everyone is basically WATCHING ME GO TO THE BATHROOM.

"I need to go home," I said. "Tryouts for regionals are in less than a *month*. If I miss more track, I'll get slower. I'm already the worst runner on the team. I can't lose speed."

"What would be so bad about getting slower?"

I gaped at her. "That means I'd be bad at track."

Why are adults so clueless?

"But if running so much has put you in the hospital, don't you think taking a break might actually be healthy? Maybe you don't *want* to make regionals."

"Of course I want to make regionals! And I'm *not* sick!" I exclaimed. (Okay, I yelled. I bet they could hear me three floors up.)

Willow didn't believe me. She told me that protesting this much is a "sign of my illness."

Willow is the *worst*.

———

Mom called tonight.

Mom *didn't* visit.

She said she had car trouble. She said I shouldn't be angry.

"I'm not mad," I said. "You're right."

It's not Mom's fault her car decided to fall apart the very night I need her the most.

It *is* her fault she took a late meeting in the first place, though. If she hadn't, maybe she could have gotten her car fixed sooner. She could have made other plans:

Mom could have taken an Uber.

Dad could have visited in her place.

Then again, I could have stopped myself from getting sick.

So sick that my parents don't want to visit me.

So sick that my best friend hates me.

Willow asked me earlier if being thin was worth all this.

"Yes," I said right away. "Of course it is." I like being skinny. I like not being made fun of for how I look. I like being faster. I like the feeling of pants slipping over my hips.

I don't like feeling this lonely, though. I don't like never being skinny enough.

I'm not sure there *is* a "skinny enough" now. "Skinny enough" is the tide going out to sea, the horizon always reaching farther back.

It was there once. Not anymore.

DAY FOUR: THURSDAY

Ali cried last night.

Ali did more crunches, too. So many that I stopped counting. The bed creaked every time she moved, and she kept gasping, like each movement hurt her. I wonder if she was pulling at her IV. I wonder if she cared.

I wonder what would happen if I did crunches, too.

Willow would be disappointed.

Mom would get mad.

I can't get the idea out of my head, though.

It's like someone drew on my brain with permanent marker, the kind you can never scrub off the sofa, no matter how hard you try.

After Ali finished her crunches, I sneezed. Ali turned over and looked at me. I squeezed my eyes closed, but I think she saw that I was awake.

I think she knows that I know.

—

I was right. Ali *does* know I heard her. She pulled me aside before breakfast, right after getting weighed. I moved away from her. I was still in that doctor's robe they make us wear, and I didn't want it to fly open in front of Ali. I don't want anyone to see my body. Not now. Not ever.

"You're not going to tell on me, right." Ali didn't say it like a question. She said it like a threat.

"What do you mean?" I stammered the words, like I used to when Talia and Camille pushed into the lunch line behind me. When they asked me questions about what I was getting, like they couldn't see right in front of their faces. When I didn't know what the right answer would ever be.

I never wanted to answer them: not until I started getting skinny.

I'm skinny now, but Ali still makes me nervous. I don't like people staring at me. I don't like people not liking me. And Ali definitely *doesn't* like me. Her eyes were narrowed and her hands were on her hips. Even her IV pole looked like it was going to attack me.

"What do I *mean*?" Ali asked. A counselor peeked out at us. Ali coughed. I smiled. Nothing going on here, la-di-da. "You know what I mean."

I looked anywhere but at Ali. At the picture of the Boston skyline on the wall. At my running shoes, which hadn't actually *run* in almost a whole week. At the rain out the window, coming down so hard I couldn't see across the courtyard.

"Last night." Ali patted her stomach and gave me a pointed look. "I know you saw me."

I started to come up with an excuse but stopped. Why bother? Ali knew I'd seen her. And maybe we could help each other.

"Fine, I saw you."

"Don't tell."

In music class last month, Mr. Chase taught us about staccato notes. Those are the ones that are short and sudden. They don't touch the notes around them. They stand apart, alone. Ali's words were like that. Ali and I are like that.

"I wouldn't tell! I'm not a tattletale!" Ali narrowed her eyes even more. "I promise!"

"You better not." Ali looked satisfied, like she was about to walk away. I jumped in before she could leave.

"How many did you do?" I asked. "I bet I used to do way more at home." Ali didn't look impressed. I wasn't going to let her beat me, though.

"Maybe I'll start doing crunches, too," I said. "If it's so easy to hide."

"Fine."

"Fine."

"Just don't get me in trouble. I'll keep your secret if you keep mine. And if you get caught, don't bring me into it. I can cry on cue. They'll never believe a thing you say."

"Fine," I said. It *was* fine, too. For the first time since I got here, my chest relaxed. It felt like someone had loosened the knots I'd been tied up in.

"We'll keep each other skinny. Deal?"

"Deal."

———

I could almost see the gears moving in Willow's head at the beginning of our session, could almost hear her therapist motor turning on. Sometimes it feels like she's asking questions right out of the textbook she had in psychology school.

"How are you feeling today?"

"What thoughts ran through your head during breakfast?"

"Are you having any problems with the other girls?"

I wanted to answer yes to her last question. I wanted to confess how scared I am of Ali. How I'm aching to do crunches tonight, but I'm also scared of getting caught. I'm scared of how guilty I'll feel afterward.

Because I know what that guilt feels like. It's how I felt every time I snuck in a run and was afraid Mom and Dad would catch me. It's the tension in my chest when I waited for Mom to find my sweaty running shorts. The sweaty palms when Dad asked me what I had for dinner at Emerson's.

I hate feeling like that. I don't *want* to feel like that anymore.

I can't help imagining myself doing crunches, though. I can't help how good I know it will feel.

I don't know if I can trust Willow to tell her everything that goes through my head. Willow with her awesome hair and her happy smile and her reassuring answers. Willow who knows all the lessons from her textbooks but doesn't know anything about how I feel.

I wanted to tell her about Ali, but I didn't.

"My parents hate me." That's what I said instead. Because even though I'm worried that Ali and Josie and Julia all hate me, I'm also worried about Mom and Dad. Maybe I could talk about that one thing with her.

One thing would be okay.

"Why do you think they hate you?" Willow starts a lot of her questions that way, like what I think is automatically wrong. Maybe she's right. Because a lot of my thoughts *don't* make sense. I *know* I'm not going to gain seven bajillion pounds if I eat a peanut butter sandwich.

But it still feels that way.

I know it's okay to have a bigger body.

But I'm still scared of changing.

I know my parents don't hate me.

But Mom sure looked like she did when she caught me on the treadmill that day.

When I got home that afternoon, the house was empty. Mom had left a note that she had a late meeting, and that Julia was down the street. Track practice had been canceled and I was freaking out. I'm usually okay with running in the rain, but that day was super windy, with lightning flashing every few minutes. I wanted to run, but I didn't want to *die*.

I got on the treadmill instead. There was a sweatshirt hanging on the side, and I made a note of exactly where it was so I could replace it when I was done. Mom was starting to catch on to my exercise schedule, and she'd made me promise to only run at practice. I promised, of course.

(I lied.)

I ran hard and fast. I upped the speed until sweat dripped off me. I thought about the project we'd done in art class that day, the one I shielded with my body so Talia wouldn't laugh at it. I thought about how upset Emerson looked when I wouldn't go over to her house that afternoon. I thought running more would make me forget. Each footfall was a word.

Too fat, too fat, too fat.

Not enough, not enough, not enough.

They're going to find out, find out, find out.

I sprinted until I gasped for breath. I wasn't bored by the hamster wheel spinning beneath me. I didn't need distractions or motivation to run. I ran because it's what I had to do.

Then Mom came down the stairs. Before I saw her, I thought I could run forever. But when I saw Mom, I pressed the big red button, the one I only press when I'm done with my miles. I *never* stop in the middle of a workout, not when I have to pee and not when I'm tired. Not for *any* reason. I *have* to finish my workouts.

I stopped for the look in Mom's eyes, though. It was anger and grief and worry and fear all wrapped up in a blue-green package.

"You. Had. A. Meeting." Each word was a gasp.

"It was canceled."

"So was track practice." I stepped onto the floor. I swayed. I caught myself. All of a sudden I wanted to curl up in a ball on the floor and have Mom give me a hug, sweat-soaked clothes and all. I wanted her to tell me that it was okay to stop, that it was okay to rest. That she'd help me, so I wouldn't have to do all this *stuff* anymore.

Instead, Mom got mad. "You lied." Her face was wooden, her words steel.

"I . . ." For a second I thought of telling her I'd bumped my head and gotten temporary amnesia. I didn't have the energy to lie, though. Not anymore. Maybe now that things were in the open, Mom could fix me.

She'd fix us.

Instead, Mom yelled about how selfish I was. How it was someone else's turn to fix me now. How she didn't "have time for this."

I'm a "this."

I don't want to be a "this." I want to be Riley.

That's the problem, though: I don't know who Riley is anymore.

What if everyone hates the real me, too?

Aisha didn't eat all her dessert at lunch. She had two cookies on her plate and only ate one, so they made her drink a Boost. We get to choose between chocolate, vanilla, or strawberry. Aisha chose chocolate. (It looked like sludge.) Heather cracked open the can and poured it into a tall glass, then brought Aisha into the hallway to drink it. She was still drinking when we filed past her on the way to group.

When Aisha came back she said it was "barftastic." (Heather yelled at her for talking about barf. It's a four-letter word around here, as bad as *diet*. Two of the girls here purge: Brenna and Laura. They *did* purge, I mean. Obviously you're not allowed to in the hospital.)

"Disgusting" is another bad word. That's what Laura called the cream sauce on her pasta last night. Jean pulled Laura out of the room, then popped back in and started blabbing about how "cream sauce tastes so much like ice cream and cheese. Yum!" She said it like we were a group of two-year-olds learning how to eat. That's what Aunt Tricia used to do with my cousin Miles when he was a baby: "Oooh, who's the little baby with the yummy-yummy corn? You are! Yes, *you are!*"

Baby talk is almost as gross as cream sauce. And who would ever believe that cream sauce tastes like ice cream? Ice cream is delicious! I can write that here because no one's going to read this. No one's going to ask me *why* I don't eat ice cream if I really like it.

Because I don't want to, that's why. Isn't that enough?

I used to eat ice cream all the time. When I was six, I asked for it for Christmas. It was the top item on my list to Santa. I dictated it to Mom and everything. She brings up the list sometimes when she's telling her "my kids are sooooo cute" stories.

I got a carton of vanilla ice cream that year. Mom probably bought herself fat-free frozen yogurt.

In Ed Group today, I learned that Ed is the one telling me I'm fat. The counselors describe Ed as a little guy living inside my head and telling me bad things about myself. A demon drawing graffiti all over my brain. A way to see my eating disorder as completely separate from me.

It sounds weird, but it kind of makes sense. That when I physically can't make myself go through the lunch line to even buy an *apple*, it's not *me* acting so weird. That deep down, there's a part of me that's still good, that still wants to do the right thing.

I like thinking that the good parts of me still exist. The counselors say that even if we don't buy the whole "Ed" thing, it's important to realize that we're not to blame. That our eating disorders didn't pop up because we're awful people, whether we starve or binge or purge.

It's in my genes, like how I have brown hair and can curl my tongue. That I was born like this, with my brain chemicals out of balance to make me more worried and anxious than other people. It's how I am.

Maybe there's no Ed, no parasite living off my insecurities and fears. Maybe this disease is just part of me, part of me that I need to triumph over and work through. Part of me that I *can* triumph over. Maybe. If I want to.

"Pretend Ed is your boyfriend," today's counselor, Gabi, told us.

We giggled when Gabi talked about boyfriends. Except for Laura, none of us have one. I can't imagine having the time for a boyfriend. Or the energy. It's already hard enough fitting in running and seeing my friends and doing homework *and* figuring out how to keep my food stuff a secret.

Plus, you're supposed to be honest with boyfriends.

Brenna got angry when Gabi started talking about boyfriends. "We could have *girlfriends*, too," she said. "People can like people of any gender. Have you lived in the world lately?" Brenna sat on the edge of her seat. She kept shifting in her chair.

I smiled at her. Meredith gave Brenna a fist bump. I know Meredith is bi, too.

Gabi told Brenna to stop moving around (*"That'll burn calories!"*), but then she apologized! She said she was sorry for assuming we were all straight and that she was proud of Brenna for speaking up for herself.

I'm not used to hearing adults admit that they're wrong. I'm not used to adults treating kids like our opinion matters.

It's nice. I like it.

"Okay, back to work," Gabi finally said. "Think about a *person* you might like." She peeked at Brenna, who gave her a thumbs-up. "Now pretend that person is mean. Cruel, even." Gabi's voice got all serious, like Ms. Moore's, my health teacher, does when she's talking about stuff like diseases and bullying. "Pretend they don't want you to hang out with your best friends anymore. They tell you what to wear and what to eat and where to go."

"That's not fair!" Rebecca exclaimed. We all jumped like someone had dropped a tray in the cafeteria. Rebecca's fists were clenched around the strings of her hoodie. A tear dripped down her cheek. "He shouldn't do that. He *can't* do that."

"He *shouldn't*," Gabi said. "But does he? And why?" Rebecca *really* started crying then. "Hold on a second, girls." Gabi pulled Rebecca aside, and they left the room for an emergency check-in. That's when the counselors do a quick one-on-one mini–therapy session with us. I haven't had one yet. I'm afraid to. It's bad enough that Willow is starting to understand how much of a mess I am. I don't want everyone else to.

I hope the check-in helped Rebecca. I'll probably never know, though. That's what happens here. We're crammed together like clowns in a minuscule car, living on top of each other and listening to each other count while we pee. We see everyone's breakdowns. We cry and have nightmares.

But the second something dramatic happens, we're told it's

none of our business. We're ordered to concentrate on our *own* recovery. We're left in the dark.

When Gabi returned, she went right back to work, with no mention of Rebecca at all. "Pretend Ed calls you names. Names like fatso and loser. He or she tells you you're weak. That you'll never amount to anything if you don't do what he or she says. That you'll never, ever be enough."

I imagined myself with a boyfriend like that. I heard insults spewing from his mouth, attaching to me like ticks. "Ed's a jerk," I said. Gabi gave me a surprised look. I haven't talked much during group so far. I don't want to say something someone will laugh at. But this time I couldn't help myself. "I'd dump him. Or her."

Gabi looked around the room. "Does everyone agree?"

Everyone else nodded.

"Of course you would. Because you don't deserve to be treated like that. Not by a boy or a girl. Not by a friend. Not by anyone." Gabi paused, probably for dramatic effect. I imagined that *dun dun DUN!* movie music in the background, the kind that plays whenever there's something important coming: A villain lurking in the shadows. A steep cliff around the corner.

A life-changing revelation.

"Then why would you let your eating disorder treat you like that? Why do you treat *yourself* like that?"

There was an alarm during dinner. The sound of running feet. Willow's voice, louder than usual. The unit door buzzed. A man who looked just like Rebecca power walked past the dining room. We had to stay in the dining room for an extra ten minutes. Gabi made us play a trivia game. I'm usually great at trivia, but I got all the answers wrong. Brenna did, too, even a super-easy one about *X-Men*.

I stared at Brenna. She stared at me. My stomach churned, but not with food this time. With fear. What was happening?

Five minutes before Gabi let us leave, Rebecca walked by. She didn't look at us. The man did, though. His face was painted with grief. He sleepwalked to the door, pulling Rebecca's suitcase behind him.

What happened to Rebecca? Was she hurt? Where is she going?

———

Everything we talk about in group makes sense. I probably *will* feel better when I gain weight. I probably *won't* hurt as much if I eat more.

It took so long to lose all this weight, though. It took so much work to make the track team. What happens if I gain it all back? I won't make regionals. I won't have my body. I don't even have art anymore.

I'll just have . . . me.

Ed might be a liar, but he makes me feel better. He makes me forget about everything else that's going on. He makes me believe, if only for a little while, that my body will be okay, even if everything else might not.

I need that. I want that.

—

We still haven't heard anything about Rebecca.

Ali thinks she had an allergic reaction to something she ate. "Everything's so gross here, I'm surprised someone doesn't get sick every day."

Brenna thinks Rebecca has family stuff going on. "Her dad looked worried. Maybe her grandmother died."

I keep wondering if it was something worse. Rebecca was so upset during group. What if there's something even more serious in her life? Maybe Rebecca is sick in other ways and needs more help than she can get here.

I hope she gets better. I hope all these girls get better. Except for Ali (who whispered "friends don't tell" at me as we were filing out of the dining room), everyone is really nice. I wish they didn't hate themselves so much. They're all pretty. Their bodies don't matter to me.

Their bodies don't matter. Mine does, though.

DAY FIVE: FRIDAY

Ali did crunches again last night. I was hoping she wouldn't, so I wouldn't have to decide whether to join her. I could already feel Ed coming to life inside my head. He was setting up camp, like we used to do when we were little, before Julia and I started complaining about how boring camping is.

For a second, I tried to think of what my healthy voice would say. They call that "positive self-talk" here. It's when you don't yell at yourself. When you encourage yourself like teammates do at track meets.

I told myself that Ali could do what she wanted and I should do what's healthy for *me*. I tried to believe all that mental cheerleading. *Go, Riley, go!*

It only lasted a second, though. Gabi made separating Ed's voice from my healthy voice sound so easy. But in real life it's impossible, because Ed sounds exactly like me. It's like how Josie's voice sounds just like her mom's. Which made it super awkward that time Mrs. Friedman answered the phone and I started blabbing about how cute we both thought Dillon Davis was. Josie didn't forgive me for like three weeks.

That was for a little *phone* mix-up, though. I don't think Josie will ever forgive me for missing her birthday party.

If I'd ignored Ed, I never *would* have missed her party.

I couldn't ignore him last night, either. I couldn't lie in bed while Ali was getting skinnier next to me. So I crunched. I crunched until I heard footsteps coming down the hall. I stopped, my heart pounding faster than it does when someone offers me a snack and I can't think of an excuse to say no. Ali and I locked eyes. She was smiling this weird congratulatory smile, like she was proud of me.

Ali looked like I always wanted Talia to look at me. Like I finally belonged. Like I wasn't Roly-Poly Riley anymore and never would be again.

Except Ali was smiling from a hospital bed. Ali was smiling while attached to an IV. Do I really want Ali's approval? Why is it so important to me?

I kept crunching until Ali stopped, though. It was a contest I couldn't lose. But now I feel so guilty. I urged Ali on, even though I know she shouldn't be doing crunches. Ali's sick. Exercise will hurt her.

So won't it hurt me, too? I'm so confused.

This is the stuff that happens all the time, the part of the eating disorder I hate. I feel good when I restrict. I feel good when I exercise. I feel *great* when I listen to that sneaky voice inside me. Only for a while, though. Then the regret comes, because I know I'm hurting myself.

I'm hurting other people, too.

It surprises me every time someone in here thinks like me. I'm so used to feeling like "the only one."

The only one who let a diet spiral into an illness.

The only one who thinks one bite of cookie will glom a zillion pounds onto my stomach.

The only one who's messed up beyond repair.

Today we had art therapy. Apparently it's a way for us to "relax and feel our emotions through art." I don't know what I think about that. I do agree that drawing makes me relax, that when I create an entire new world on paper I can forget about my own.

Except I *don't* want to feel my emotions. Not in regular therapy and not in art therapy. I don't want to talk about what scares me.

We didn't have to talk today, though. We just drew.

"Today I want you to draw someone you love," Zelda, the art therapist, said. "Picture them in your mind and put them on paper."

Meredith started to protest that she was the "worst artist ever," but Zelda cut her off. "I don't care if you're not good at this. You can draw something abstract if you want. You can scribble like a little kid. But I do want you to do the work. I want you to think about that person and what they look like. Then, around your drawing, I want you to write words you associate with them. What do you love about that person? What makes them special?"

Everyone else got to work right away. I finally decided to draw Josie, probably because I can't stop thinking about her. I drew her wavy hair and her brown eyes. I drew her short legs and her favorite jeans, the ones with the rips in the knees.

Around her, I wrote a cloud of compliments:

Good listener.

Silly.

Laughs at my jokes.

Asks to see my drawings.

Loves hiking.

Great at science.

"What's more important?" Zelda asked when we were done. "The body itself? Or what makes the person *inside* that body so special?"

I stared at my drawing. Zelda's right. I don't care what Josie looks like. I do care what *I* look like, though, even if I shouldn't. That's why the next part of Zelda's assignment will be impossible. She asked us to draw *ourselves*.

"I don't want you to draw your bodies, but I *do* want you to draw your faces. Draw yourself as you look when you're the happiest. When you're content and accepting of yourself. Capture that feeling and think about what makes you that way."

"But I'm *not* accepting of myself," Laura said.

"I don't *want* to draw myself," Brenna said. "Even if it's just my face. I'm way bigger than everyone here."

But you're beautiful.

I wanted to say that to Brenna, but I knew she wouldn't listen.

Because *I* wouldn't have listened to me, either. I *don't* listen to me.

Brenna's not the only one who doesn't think she's beautiful. I'm not the only one who criticizes herself. We're all messed up. Even though sometimes I don't feel like I belong here, it's nice to get reminders that I'm not the only one who feels like I'm drowning.

Like I'm flailing in the middle of the ocean with two life rafts in front of me: one will save me and the other will deflate the second I grab it. One life raft is recovery. The other life raft is staying sick. I just don't know which is which.

Maybe everyone else wonders this, too. When I hear them crying at night, maybe they're as scared as I am. We're all sick. But will we all get well? Will *I* get well?

Willow says that's up to me.

I know I'm strong. I worked hard and made the track team. I worked hard and lost weight. I *could* work hard and recover. I could eat food. I could rest. I could hang out with my friends and be a normal kid.

Maybe I could.

DAY SIX: SATURDAY

I shouldn't have eaten breakfast.

I want to go for a run. I need to go for a run. I can't go for a run.

I hate my flip-flopping brain. Didn't I tell it that I might want to get better? Last night, when I was lying in bed, I even thought that maybe I'd hit that "turning point" everyone talks about, the moment when I realize that life *without* anorexia is better than life with it.

Then Ali started doing crunches. At first I told myself that I wouldn't join her. Then Ali whispered across the room, her words bobbing in the air between our beds. "You're doing them, too, right?"

I wanted to say no, but her face was a threat.

You can't back out now, it said.

I wanted to say no, but her words were a challenge.

Don't be weak, they said.

My mind swirled like a whirlpool pulling me in. Willow says that strength is standing up to the eating disorder. My head says that strength is movement, strength is giving in.

I tried to use the Ed/Healthy Voice dialogue they taught us, but it didn't work.

> **Ed:** *You don't want to be a failure.*
>
> **Healthy Voice:** *I'm not a failure. Resisting my urge to exercise is a victory!*
>
> **Ed:** *Doing nothing when you could be doing crunches is a failure, too. You can't get out of shape. You have to make regionals!*
>
> **Healthy Voice:** *I need to get healthy. I need to gain weight.*
>
> **Ed:** *Julia's skinny and she's healthy.*
>
> **Healthy Voice:** *Julia's different than me.*
>
> **Ed:** *Julia is different than you. She's better. Stronger. So is Ali.*

I did the crunches, but now I want to cry. For a little while yesterday, I imagined what life might be like without these thoughts running through my head every second of every day. I thought I could be okay.

I was wrong.

Why is this so hard? I want to be better. I don't want to be sad anymore.

I got an e-mail from Emerson! Finally!

Riley!!!

I miss you tons. Track is boring without you. Talia keeps bragging that she's going to win the 400 in our meet next week. She might, but only because you're not here. You rock at the 400!

I think Tommy is going to ask me to the Spring Dance. He keeps staring at me in science class. At first I thought it was because my hair was sticking up, but when I checked, my hair looked awesome. So I think he likes me.

Jacob already asked Talia to the dance. Like a "date." She's bragging about how they're going to dinner before at a fancy restaurant. That sounds boring. I'd rather get a hamburger and fries.

I miss you! School isn't the same without you!

Hugs,
Emerson

Jacob asked Talia to the dance. Of course he did. Talia's perfect. Talia's skinny. Talia isn't so clumsy that she drops her notebooks in the hallway. Talia doesn't get tongue-tied when Jacob tries to help her pick up her papers.

I wish Emerson hadn't told me about Jacob. I wish she hadn't told me about track or the dance. It reminds me of what I'm missing now *and* what I missed before.

I wish I had a magic wand that could send me back in time. I'd laugh during track practice instead of thinking about burning calories. I wouldn't skip our weekly sleepovers to avoid the Chinese food Emerson's mom always orders. I'd go to Josie's birthday party no matter what. Even if I had to eat two whole pizzas myself. Two whole pizzas with pepperoni and the greasiest cheese in the universe. Cheese so greasy that it drips from my fingers like slime.

I'd eat slimy cheese to get Josie back in my life.

I sent Josie an e-mail before my computer time was over.

Josie,

I'm sorry. I'm so, so sorry. I know I've said it before, but I need to say it again. I was a bad friend. I made a mistake. Please don't punish me anymore. Let me make it up to you.

Love and hearts,
Riley

I finally talked about my friends during today's session with Willow. I told her how Emerson and I were in a baby playgroup together. How Josie and I were in the same kindergarten class and fought over the orange blocks until the teacher persuaded us to share the red and yellow blocks so we could "make orange together."

How Emerson convinced me to try out for her track team after I didn't make the art show. How running made me forget about how untalented I was. How I got better, but Emerson is always faster, no matter how hard I try.

How Josie does Girl Scouts and is into science experiments. How I kept her secret when she peed the bed sleeping over at my house in fourth grade and she's the only one who knows that when I was in first grade, I wanted to marry Clifford the Big Red Dog. We planned a wedding between me and a huge stuffed animal and Josie has never made fun of me for it. *That's* being a good friend.

"*I'm* not a good friend, though." I started crying, right in front of Willow. Huge tears that plopped onto my cheeks and rolled onto my shirt. Willow gave me a tissue and waited. She didn't laugh at me, like Camille did when I teared up after the BMI testing. She didn't tell me to stop crying like Dad does when I'm not being "positive enough." I think that's why I was honest—completely honest—about what happened with Josie.

I skipped Josie's thirteenth birthday party. The thirteenth birthday party that I helped organize. That I sent out the invitations for and helped decorate for *and* picked out the food for.

I wanted to go. I'd been to every single one of Josie's parties since we'd met. I'd slept over after them, too. But I couldn't be there this year, even though everyone knows that thirteen is the *most important birthday ever.*

Because when Emerson and I went shopping, she made me buy everything I'm scared of: Cheese puffs. Those chocolate-chip cookies from the bakery that melt in your mouth. M&M's. Ingredients for the make-your-own pizzas Josie was so excited about. Ice cream.

It all looked so good. It all looked so bad.

So I pretended to be sick.

At first I tried to be brave. I ran extra the day before, so I could let myself eat "normally" at the party. Then I spent the whole *night* before imagining how it would feel to eat all that yummy stuff. How I would feel *after* I ate all that stuff.

I couldn't sleep. I kept weighing myself instead.

I called Josie an hour before the party. I coughed a lot and made my voice sound all weak. I told her I'd been sick ALL DAY LONG. She was disappointed, but I knew she'd get over it. Then stupid Mom went to the stupid party to pick me up. Because I'd been the stupidest person in the whole stupid world and forgotten to tell *Mom* (who had been at work) that I was "sick." And Mom told Josie that of course I wasn't sick, I'd gone for a run just that morning!

Busted.

I didn't have to eat the pizza or those yummy cookies, but I lost one of my best friends. And right now, I'd rather have Josie than be this skinny. I'd eat *ten* cookies just to hear her giggling over a silly kitten meme or to read one of her texts.

"So you'd eat ten cookies to get Josie back?" Willow asked me.

I nodded. "I'd do *anything* to have Josie back."

"What else would you like in your life? Or out of it?"

We brainstormed.

1. Art without stress.
2. No more calorie counting.
3. Running for fun. (Or maybe no running at all.)
4. Sleepovers.
5. Ice cream. Pizza. Sandwiches. Cake. Peanut butter. (I stopped myself from spending an hour listing foods.)
6. Maybe a future as an artist? (I said this really quickly, in case Willow said I was being silly. She didn't say I was being silly.)

I kept wanting to make snarky comments to Willow. I kept wanting to tell her that the life we were describing wasn't realistic. That *no one* is that happy.

I wasn't a brat, though. I "worked at therapy," as they say here. I told myself that for one session, it was okay to believe that I *could* get that life one day. Willow believes I can be that person, too. She even told me how to get there. It's the answer I've been avoiding this whole time.

"So if you'd eat cookies to get Josie back, can you take things one step further? Can you eat your meal plan and recover to get your life back?" she asked me.

I think I can. I think I want to.

(Oh my god, is this place actually working?)

———

Ali's in a check-in now. I bet she's complaining about how her parents are coming to visit today. Ali says her parents spend too much time with her. They ask too many questions about her life. They want her to eat all her meals with them. (Except for that last part, it sounds kind of nice.)

Maybe I should use a check-in, too. I can't stop jiggling my legs. I already got yelled at for it three times. They think I'm trying to burn extra calories. I'm not; I just feel like my heart is going to burst out of my chest. Like my skin's too tight on my body.

Mom and Julia are visiting today, too.

Mom promised she'd be here. "No matter what," she said on the phone. "Even if my car breaks down and I have to rent—no, buy!—a limousine. Or a jumbo jet. I'll be there."

"I'm sure the hospital has a helipad on the roof."

I imagined Mom landing a helicopter on the roof, and I laughed. The laugh bubbled to the surface like something rising from the ocean. A shipwreck, revealing itself after years buried at sea.

A treasure.

———

I'm so bored. Brenna has been gone all day. We get to do that once we've been here awhile and are "making progress." Brenna's going to see a movie and get ice cream. She didn't seem that nervous, but I'm totally freaking out for her. Ice cream is scary. It's so good, though. I can almost taste an Oreo cone now. That's what I used to order at Sully's Ice Cream Stand: two scoops of Oreo with rainbow sprinkles. Yum.

Brenna brought a book with her, in case the movie is boring. I've never heard of anyone doing that before.

"Isn't it too dark to read?" I asked her.

"Not if I use my flashlight app."

"Doesn't your mom get upset you're not paying attention? Or complain that the light is distracting?" That's what my mom would do. She'd say that we paid good money for the movie and it's our responsibility as social citizens to set a good example in the movie theater.

Something like that. As long as people don't think we're doing anything "wrong" or "improper," Mom is happy. I'm still not sure who these "people" are. Mom is always super worried about what they think, though.

What if the critics don't like my new show?

What if Julia's leotards are more faded than all her teammates'?

What if my boss sees you and notices how skinny you are?

Mom's head is as busy as mine.

I guess Brenna's mom isn't like that, though. Because Brenna shrugged and said her mom doesn't care as long as Brenna's quiet during the movie.

"She's in all these movie fanatic groups online and watches the Oscars like my dad watches the World Series. Mom doesn't like to miss a second of any movie." Brenna rolled her eyes. "That means she drags me to see all the serious and boring ones."

I agreed that a book is way better than sitting through all that. Especially the one Brenna is reading, a graphic novel called *All's Faire in Middle School*. I wonder if the author of that book drew when she was a kid like me. I wonder if *she* was bad once, too.

———

Mom and Julia came! They didn't even have to rent a helicopter. They were here at the very start of visiting hours, too, which is so not like Mom. She's always late. But today she wasn't!!!

It's little, but it's something.

When Julia sat down on my bed, her eyes wandered around the room, from the bare walls to the scratched dresser to the locked bathroom door. I don't know if she was judging me, but *I* was judging me. I'm supposed to be the big sister. I'm supposed to be someone Julia looks up to, someone who's grown-up. I feel like a total baby, though, one step away from someone wiping me after I pee.

Maybe that's why I snapped at Mom when she asked me how I was doing.

"How do you *think* I'm doing?" I didn't tell her how I might want to get better now. I didn't tell her how I wasn't mad at her for sticking me in here anymore.

Because all of a sudden I *was* mad. I was mad that Julia is skinny and athletic and healthy. I was mad that I'm stuck in these cement walls where counselors tell me what to do and where to go. I was mad that Dad didn't come. I was mad that Mom was probably going to leave and go right back to work, even though it's a Saturday, because *that's what she always does*.

"You don't have to be so mean, Riley." Julia's lip trembled, but I bet she was totally faking. Julia is the master at fake crying. She tears up when Dad says she can't go to a PG-13 movie, then stops crying the second he changes his mind.

"Riley, be nice to your sister."

Just like that, the old Mom was back. The one who blames

me instead of Julia. The one who notices I'm angry but doesn't ask me *why*. At least this time she caught herself and gave me a hug.

I pulled away from her. I don't want Mom feeling how skinny I am. I don't want Mom feeling how fat I am.

"Let me give you a tour!" The words came out in my fake cheery voice, the one I used at school when teachers asked me if I was okay with those concerned looks on their faces. The one I used at home until Mom and Dad found out the truth and everything fell apart.

When I showed them the dining room, Julia asked why my name wasn't up on the wall under the picture of Elsa.

"I haven't graduated yet. Or been discharged. Whatever they call it here." I picked up one of the snowflakes and tried to imagine what I'd write on it eventually, what I'd "let go" of.

My worry about getting fat? I'd like to do that.

Being so lonely? I'd like to do that, too.

Can I do it, though? It seems impossible.

In the group room, Julia asked if she could use the art supplies. She drew me a picture of a hydrangea, her favorite flower. Aunt Tricia's beach house on Cape Cod has hydrangea bushes all over the front yard. When Julia was little, she couldn't say *hydrangea*, so she just called them "pretty." Aunt Tricia's yard had "yulips and rosies and pretties."

I drew a picture of Julia. I should have tried to draw my face again, but every time I try, my hand won't move. I don't want to put any more evidence of what I look like out in the world. The picture of Julia came out pretty good, though. Her nose was only partially messed up.

Mom even asked if she could bring it home. "I've always loved your drawings," she said. She didn't say anything about how silly it looked. She didn't say anything about my use of color or shading or how good I used to be. She just folded it carefully and put it in her purse, tucked into the pages of a book so it wouldn't get wrinkled.

I put Julia's flower on my wall.

I like to think that even if Mom wouldn't put my drawing in her gallery, at least she'd put it on the fridge. That's what she used to do with our finger paintings. We wrote our names on the bottom: my RILEY always had the L backward. Julia always switched around the I and the A.

I was proud of my art back then. Mom was proud of my art.

Maybe someday we can both be proud of it again.

———

Tonight during free time, we decorated Ali's IV pole so it looked like a person. Brenna grabbed a hat someone's visitor had left and put it on top, then Laura wrapped one of her sweaters around it.

(Laura has something like ten sweaters here. I need to ask Mom for more. This place is freezing.)

Meredith drew a mad face on the bag of fluid with a marker. (She got into trouble for doing it, too. She had to eat her evening snack in a separate room for "tampering with medical equipment.") I don't think Meredith cared, though. Because tonight was so much fun!

For the first time since I got here, I didn't feel like I was in the middle of a nightmare. We were just a bunch of girls goofing off together. Ali made fake feet out of construction paper and painted the toenails pink. Brenna wheeled Ali and her IV pole around and pretended to dance with them. Laura took a turn, then taught us all to waltz. (Her mom is a ballroom dance teacher!) I partnered with Meredith, who made me feel like a total oaf. When (if?) she recovers, she's going to be an awesome ballerina.

Aisha grabbed a lion mask off the wall, one someone probably made in art therapy years ago, then held it in front of her face and asked the IV pole questions about itself, like she was a news reporter and it was her subject. She kept roaring, too. It was the funniest thing I've seen in forever.

For a few minutes, I almost forgot where I was. It was just me and a bunch of my friends. And here's the weird thing—these girls are starting to *feel* like my friends, even though I just met them a week ago. (Okay, not Ali. But I'm trying to forget about her. She hasn't been that bad today.)

I thought that treatment was going to be awful. I thought everyone would make fun of me, like they do at school.

I'm starting to realize that the awful part was *before*, though. The worries and the obsessions, the scales and the nutrition labels. The running and moving and hating.

Dressing up an IV pole may be silly. Talking about my feelings might be cheesy (extra-cheese-pizza-level cheesy). But I'm happier than I was before. I like myself more. I'm drawing more.

Maybe I'm not in the middle of a nightmare, after all.

DAY EIGHT: MONDAY

Laura tried to throw up after breakfast. I was walking past the bathroom and Heather was standing outside, scrolling through her phone. Laura was counting inside the bathroom. After she said "thirteen," the counting stopped.

All the staff have bathroom keys on colored bracelets around their wrists. Heather's is bright pink. She ripped that bracelet off superfast and threw open the bathroom door. I know I shouldn't have peeked inside, but I did. It's not like I *wanted* to see Laura, but I couldn't help it—the door was open. She was bent over the toilet, her curtain of hair hanging down to cover her face. Laura didn't even stop when Heather got near her.

I wonder if Laura got barf on her hair. Gross.

I ran into the group room then. I didn't tell anyone, but everyone still found out. There's no way to keep a secret in this place. I haven't seen Laura since. I wonder if she got kicked out. I wonder if she's going to the same place Rebecca did. I still wonder where Rebecca is. I wonder if I'll ever find out.

I've never purged before. It always seemed gross to me. But it'd be nice to be empty inside.

I miss being empty. Being hungry. Light. Clean.

But it's nice to be full, too. My stomach doesn't hurt as much anymore. I eat and I digest. It's almost like my body is doing what it was meant to do.

———

In group today, we talked about self-esteem. Sixty minutes of why we're so wonderful the way we are and how our bodies were made "to be, not do." Sixty minutes of affirmation after affirmation. (Which are basically brags you're allowed to say.) The counselor made us go around in a circle and say something we loved about ourselves.

Ali said she was a good friend. (I tried not to laugh when she said that.)

Brenna said she had a nice laugh. (She does! It's deep and vibrates through the room.)

Laura said she liked her fingernail polish. (I wasn't sure that counted, but no one said anything.)

I went last. I couldn't think of anything for like five whole minutes. Okay, it was really only five seconds, but it felt way longer. Especially since I was blushing. "My pale skin" is definitely *not* something I like about myself.

I haven't been a good friend lately. Or a good sister. Probably not a good daughter, either.

I finally blurted out that I liked the birthmark on my ankle. Everyone stared at my ankle, which was covered up by my sock. "It looks like a heart," I explained.

We had to do some worksheet after that, where we listed things we hate about being sick. It made me feel like I'm in school again. Weirdly, it made me *miss* school.

It even made me miss homework.

DAY NINE: TUESDAY

I'm so hungry. I eat more in one meal now than I used to in one day. Why am I hungry? I shouldn't be hungry.

When I was at home and hunger pains clenched my stomach in their fists, there was a mantra I recited to myself: *Strong, stronger, strongest.*

I chanted it until my mind was focused enough to conquer my body. Until the glasses of water and the cans of diet soda and the constant running quieted the grumbling inside. Until everything stopped hurting so much.

Strong, stronger, strongest.

My body yelled that it needed calories and energy. It begged me to listen. But I thought I could conjure energy out of thin air, out of sprints and sit-ups, starvation and failed attempts at sleep.

I did conjure energy for a while. I was in control. I made magic. I was stronger than the pain. My mantra isn't helping me in here, though. There's nothing to fight back against. They won't let me be hungry. They've taken my eating disorder away. It's trapped inside my brain, screaming for freedom.

When I tell it I want the noise in my head to stop, it gets louder.

When I tell it I want to get better, it tells me I'm weak.

I tell myself that I'm not my body, that I'm strong enough to beat this. I tell myself so many things, but I'm still scared. I don't know if I'm brave enough to make it to the finish line.

—

I want to tell Willow how I've been doing crunches. She says I need to be honest for her to really help me.

In our last session, Willow talked about "accountability" and how my eating disorder thrives on secrets. "Imagine planting a seed in the ground," she said.

I made a joke about being an awful gardener and how I killed the birthday rosebush Grandma gave me last year. Willow smiled, but she didn't laugh.

"This is important," she said. "If you water and give that seed food, it will grow. If you give it sunlight, it will thrive." Willow pointed to the plant on her desk, the one that's green and lush. "This plant is like your eating disorder."

"Huh?"

"Eating disorders thrive on secrets," Willow said. "Secrets make them grow. Deception makes them strong. If you don't give your eating disorder what it wants, if you ignore it and starve it—instead of yourself—it will die. The seed will stay a seed."

"So it's good that I'm a plant killer?" I joked again.

This time Willow did laugh. "It's a start," she said. "Just remember that I won't judge you. I *want* to hear your secrets so we can deal with them together."

I *want* to confess, but every time I try, the words skulk back into the shadows, ducking and hiding behind my shame.

> **Ed:** *If you tell Willow, she'll get mad at you. She'll make you stop.*
>
> **Healthy Voice:** *But I want to stop. And right now, I can't stop myself.*
>
> **Ed:** *If you tell Willow, she'll be disappointed in you. Everyone will.*
>
> **Healthy Voice:** *If I tell Willow, she'll be proud of me for telling the truth. She'll help me get better.*
>
> **Ed:** *You don't want to get better.*
>
> **Healthy Voice:** *Maybe I do.*

———

Ali got her IV out this morning. I guess she's hydrated enough to not need it. Or nutrient-full enough. She's still full of mean, though. This morning she told me I looked healthy. She had this annoying half smile on her face when she said it, because we both knew what she meant.

"Healthy" doesn't mean that I'm not sick.

"Healthy" means that I'm fat.

That all my fears are coming true. That even with the crunches, I'm gaining weight in here. I'm gaining *too much* weight in here.

Ali's comment made me not want to eat. It made me want to tell the counselors that I'm done with this, that I need to leave.

What's *wrong* with me? I say I want to recover. I wrote yesterday that I don't want to be sick anymore. But I'm still scared of gaining weight. I'm still doing crunches. I'm still keeping secrets.

And what's wrong with gaining weight anyway? We talked about that in group this morning, how the world thinks fat is the worst thing ever, worse than disease and pollution and even *death*.

"People call me all sorts of names," Brenna said. "They make fun of me because I'm fat. When I told my soccer team I was going in here, half the kids laughed because they didn't believe someone like me could get an eating disorder."

"You're not fat," I said quickly.

"I *am* fat," Brenna said. "I'm fat because that's how I was made. I'm not meant to be skinny like you, Riley. And not just because I binge. Because I'm me." She looked to Heather for approval, like her words could break into pieces at any moment.

"You're right, Brenna," Heather said. "What's so bad about fat anyway?"

No one answered.

"Does being skinny make you a better person?"

"Does eating less food make you more kind?"

"Is eating too much food a crime?"

It feels that way.

"That's what we want you to realize in here." Heather's voice rose like she was onstage giving a speech. "You're *all* meant to live in different bodies, bodies you'll naturally have without stuffing or starving or punishing yourselves. You may end up in a body that's fat. You may end up in a body that's muscular or thin, curvy or straight up and down.

"It will be *your* body, though. Your body that you live in and love in and play in. You can still have friends in that body. You can still have fun in that body. You can still live your life in that body. Because you are so much more than your size."

"I don't want to be fat," Ali said.

Brenna glared at her. I glared at Ali, too. I still think the same thing a little bit, but Heather makes sense. Wouldn't I rather be fat than miserable?

Ali didn't notice our glares. I bet she forgot everything Heather said. Because right now she's dancing around the group room, waving her arms and wiggling her hips. "No IV, no IV!" She's chanting it like she's a cheerleader. Everyone else is giggling. Everyone else likes Ali. No one else sees what a faker she is.

I used to want to be like Ali. I don't think I do anymore.

Brenna's words keep echoing in my head: *I'm not meant to be skinny like you, Riley.*

Am I meant to be skinny? Yeah, I'm skinny *now*, but I only look this way because I'm sick. When I recover, I'll look different. I may *not* be skinny.

I'll still be me, though.

And I think that's a good thing.

———

I got mail today! Two things, actually. One was a postcard from Julia. I laughed when I saw it, because it reminded me of the summer when I was nine and Julia was eight. That's the year Mom was between jobs and Julia was starting to get serious about gymnastics. She didn't have practice every day, so it was okay to go to Cape Cod for a week.

Okay to spend every day at the beach instead of in the gym.

Okay to splash in the waves without worrying about what my body looked like.

Okay not to have to wear a two-piece to be cool.

Okay to eat ice cream twice a day.

Okay to have fun.

That's the summer Julia and I went to the country store around the corner from our rented cottage and picked out postcards to send to everyone back home. We tried to find the silliest pictures: the lobster with one eye bigger than the other, the sea otter in sunglasses, Santa fishing on the end of a pier.

Today I got a postcard from Julia. It had a big blue whale on the front, with GET WHALE SOON in bright yellow letters. On the back she wrote: *I miss you. I hope you're home soon.* The postcard made me happy. Because Julia was thinking about me. Because Julia didn't hate me for being such an awful sister.

The other thing I got was a letter from Emerson. It was super short, just a bunch of stuff about track and school and tests and how I'm *so* lucky I missed our unit on Industrialization last week because it was *so* boring.

The best part wasn't Emerson's letter, though. It's what was in the envelope *with* the letter: a newspaper clipping. It reminded me of the letters Grandma Archibald sends us, with an "only funny to old people" comic from the newspaper attached or an article about how important sunscreen is.

Emerson's clipping was about an art class at the community center, one that starts next month.

I'll do it with you. It'll be fun! Emerson wrote on the bottom, next to a big smiley face.

Emerson didn't write anything about me being sick. She wrote to me like I was a regular person, someone who used to love art. Someone who could maybe love it again.

I keep thinking about that class. It's scary to think of someone looking at my drawings. But Mom won't be there to criticize them. *And* I've been drawing more the past few days. Not televisions, and not even my usual dragons and animals. I've been drawing more people, like we did that time in art therapy. I still haven't been able to draw *my* face, but I drew Brenna's. Aisha's, too. I used pencil and worked on shadow and light.

I think they're okay.

I think *I'm* okay.

Maybe I could get better.

———

Brenna's definitely my best friend in the hospital. Last night we did a puzzle in the group room before bed. There was a picture of a kitten with fairy wings on the box, but the inside was full of pieces from all different puzzles. So we pieced together what we called a "mutant puzzle." There were pieces with cars and trucks, pieces with a mermaid, and pieces of the Eiffel Tower. The final result looked hilarious.

I bet in real life I'd be friends with Brenna.

This isn't real life, though.

When I get out of here, I'll probably never see her again. Brenna will live her life and I'll live mine. The hospital will be a memory.

I wonder if that day will ever come, when I barely remember these walls and this hospital food. When I'm so happy that I forget what it's like to be this scared.

Tonight I asked Brenna if she was happy. They talk a lot about being happy here. Happy with our bodies. Happy with who we are. Happy with our life. I never feel happy, though, not all the way. I'm always waiting for something to go wrong. *Are* there people who are happy all the time? Is that even realistic?

Brenna shrugged. "I guess. I'm happier than I was before. At least I know I'm not the only one like this." She pulled at her pixie cut. "I'm annoyed with my hair, though. It's growing out so weird."

I need a haircut, too. They don't have a stylist at the hospital. We don't even have hair dryers. Hair isn't a huge deal to me, though, not as much as it is for Brenna. She says she feels more herself when her hair is short, that long hair makes her feel fake.

"When I have long hair, I feel like I'm playing a part. And I only like playing parts when I'm cosplaying." We giggled. Brenna showed me pictures of her at Comic-Con. She dressed up as Batgirl *and* as a steampunk Cinderella. She won an award for the Cinderella costume and took pictures with tons of famous people!

Brenna doesn't hide as much of herself as I do.

Brenna's way braver than me.

"But how can you be happy when you're still big?" Whoops. That came out wrong. I didn't mean that.

Did I mean that?

Brenna bit her lip. Her shoulders slumped.

"I'm sorry! I didn't mean there's anything wrong with your size. I'm an awful person." Apologies flew from my mouth like

Silly String from a can. Why would I say something like that? I don't care about weight. I don't *want* to care about weight.

Brenna took a deep breath. "No, it's okay. It's okay," she repeated, like she was reassuring herself. "It's okay. I *am* bigger than you. And even though I've stopped bingeing in here, I don't think I've lost much weight." Another breath. "That's okay, though. I guess I'm realizing *this* is who I am."

Brenna gestured down at her body. "And that this isn't *all* I am. Plus, eating gets easier with time. Your body will feel better with time. I promise." Her eyes brightened. "Plus, now that I'm doing better, my dad is planning a trip to Disney World this summer. I can't go if I'm still sick. I can't do Comics Club at school, either."

That's what I've been realizing, too: How much I've been missing out on. How much I'm *going* to miss if I stay sick. If/when I recover, I can take that art class. I can have fun at sleepovers and go to school dances. (Even though school dances are totally silly. They have them after school in the cafeteria. Where we just ate lunch three hours ago and where it still smells of overcooked green beans. Three hours and a few rolls of streamers do *not* cover up the stink of green beans.)

"I'm still nervous about food, but I'm not miserable," Brenna said. "I don't want to throw up or binge as much, and I'm actually excited about things now."

"Does that mean you're recovered?" I asked her.

Brenna laughed. "Yeah, right. Did you see me this morning?"

We laughed. Brenna cried this morning when they gave her a bagel instead of an English muffin. People lose it over random stuff in here. Last night Aisha had a panic attack because her slice of cake had more frosting than Meredith's. Meredith went around all smug for the next hour until Aisha told on her.

"Willow says it'll be like that for a while," Brenna said. "Up and down. One step forward, two steps back. But to focus on the good things. How the bad parts and the sad parts are so much smaller."

"That's what she told me, too," I said. "That eventually it'll be two steps forward and *one* step back."

"We just have to keep walking." We said this at the same time, which cued up a massive gigglefest. Willow repeats herself a lot. I think that's another thing they learn in therapist school.

"It's still hard," Brenna whispered. "I still compare myself to other people."

"I wish I could be small forever."

"But is it worth it?"

Is it? That's what I have to figure out, I guess.

Brenna and I stopped talking for a minute while Laura rummaged around the craft closet. She left with watercolors, charcoals, and construction paper. Laura's pretty good at art. Maybe even better than me. I'm not jealous, though. (At least I keep telling myself not to be.)

"You asked how I can be so happy?" Brenna asked. "It's because I pretend. Not *all* the time, but some of the time. Pretending that things are okay makes me feel brave. Remembering how awful my life was before helps me move forward. Being here makes me feel stronger. It makes me feel safe."

Then she turned away and started reading her book. She's reading one I read last year—*Goodbye Stranger* by Rebecca Stead. It's about a bunch of girls and *their* problems with growing up.

It's weird to hear someone talk about the hospital being a safe place. Brenna's right, though. I do feel safe here. They make me eat here. They make me rest. They teach us to remember what's good about our lives and help us be strong while our minds are buzzing with anxiety. They're the mallets in that whack-a-mole game that I'm so bad at, banging at our fears the second they come to the surface.

There are a lot of moles in my head.

It's nice to know that even if Brenna *does* pretend sometimes, she's still doing okay. I'm going to try to pretend, too. Maybe I won't be happy all the time. Maybe I won't have some blissfully perfect life. Maybe I'll still have problems.

But a little happiness is better than none.

DAY TEN: WEDNESDAY

"Let's talk about your family."

Willow's greeting made my chest squeeze like there was a python wrapped around me. A python forcing out words instead of air, words that I want to keep inside where it's dark. Inside where they can stay hidden.

I don't *want* to talk about my family.

I want to eat the hospital food, listen to their lectures, and do this whole recovery thing. I want to snap my fingers so—*TA-DA!*—everything will be better.

I don't need to *talk* to do that.

Willow thinks I do, though. Willow loves to talk. I bet Willow goes home and talks to herself. If she's married, I bet she talks to her husband until he puts in earplugs. I bet she talks to her dog.

I don't want her to talk to *me*.

Except we did talk, because after two whole minutes of quiet, I *had* to say something. That's one thing I've realized over the last week—it's way worse to sit in silence than to open my mouth. (And I hate to admit it, but I *do* feel better when I leave Willow's office.)

"I don't like my family."

I expected Willow's eyes to open wide in shock. I expected her to tell me that I was an awful daughter, that my parents were paying for my treatment and how dare I not like them?

She didn't say any of that. Willow took a sip of water. That's all the counselors are allowed to drink around us. No soda, no juice, no coffee or tea. Just water. They can't eat, either, even when *we're* eating *our* meals. Aisha thinks they only eat meals at the beginning and the end of the day, like her family does during Ramadan—that their time here is one big fast. *I* like to imagine they're robots who plug into charging cables at set times for their nutrients.

At least my Willow Robot has emotions. Because she didn't act like I was a selfish, ungrateful jerk. She told me it's okay to feel the way I feel. I've never heard *anyone* say that before.

"Whatever you tell me stays in this room," Willow said. "I won't tell anyone. I promise."

I'm still not sure I believe her. I wonder if my confessions are written in that folder with my name on it. I wonder if everyone looks at them and talks about me. I wondered, but I still talked. I couldn't keep it inside any longer.

"I don't know what I can do." I felt like I was going to cry. I feel like that a lot in here. Willow says it's because I'm not pushing down my emotions with all the distractions of the eating disorder.

"Do about what?"

"I don't know what I can do to make my parents love me." That's when I broke down. I cried those ugly tears that plop everywhere like raindrops. The tears that leave my eyes red and blotchy. The ones I cried in the bathroom every time Talia and her crew made fun of me.

"Why don't you think they love you?" Willow didn't look at me like I was a loser, but I still felt like one.

"They sent me here like I'm some criminal who robbed a store. Mom's only visited me one time. Dad doesn't call because he thinks I'm broken. Julia's the special one. Julia's the one they want."

I started crying again, and Willow leaned over to hug me. I'm not sure if she's *supposed* to do that, but it felt nice.

"Do you think your parents are scared?"

It was a question I've never thought about before. I never think about my parents' feelings. I mean, I think about how they get mad at me. How Dad loves building stuff and Mom helped campaign during the last presidential election. But I never think about the deep-down feelings, the ones that make Mom and Dad real people.

"About what?" I asked. "I mean, they worry about money a lot. They pay for Julia's gymnastics stuff, and I guess the hospital costs a lot, too."

"What about *you*, though?" Willow asked. "Do you think

they're scared about you?" I must have looked confused, because Willow kept talking. "Scared you're going to die?"

"I'm not going to die."

"You could." Willow's nice therapist expression turned serious. She looked like my teachers do when no one's done the assigned reading. "People die from eating disorders, Riley. It happens. It's happened in here."

I felt like I'd been punched in the stomach.

"I don't want to die," I said. "I won't. Everything's fine."

That's what I always said to Mom and Dad. *Everything's fine.* I never believed myself, though. I bet they never believed me, either. What if they *are* afraid I'm going to die? What if they worry about me as much as they cheer for Julia?

"Maybe that's why your dad is so scared to talk to you," Willow said gently. "Maybe he's afraid of what's happening. Maybe he's afraid of making things worse."

I thought about how Dad flinches away from me like a scared rabbit. The way he pauses before he says anything, like his words are flames and I'm a pile of kindling. I thought about how we used to watch Pixar movies together and act out our favorite scenes. How he used to ride the bike path with me and always let me beat him when we raced.

I thought about Mom, how she let me dust the pictures in her old gallery, even though it was probably against the rules, because I told her I wanted to be "just like her." How she came to my first track meet, even though she was late. How she read me a chapter of Harry Potter every night for years, even when she was on a business trip and we had to FaceTime.

How she researched *how* to help me and sent me to a place where I *could* be helped.

"Maybe they *do* love me?"

"Maybe they can love two daughters at the same time?"

"Then why is gymnastics the most important thing in the world? Why did I have to quit art because I wasn't good enough?"

Willow paused, letting me know that something very important and very therapist-y was coming. "Did your parents tell you to quit art?"

"Yes! Well, no. I mean . . ."

Then our time was up. Jean knocked on the door and told Willow it was time for me to eat lunch. I left the office. Willow left me with questions.

Did Mom tell me to quit art? Did *anyone* tell me my drawings weren't good enough? Or is that something I told myself? Did I quit before I could even get better?

———

Mom *did* want to help me, no matter how angry she looked after the Great Lasagna Catastrophe. That's what I call the follow-up to the Treadmill Incident. It was what made Mom finally break down and call the hospital.

Okay, I know I shouldn't have thrown a fit because Mom used

the full-fat mozzarella cheese. But I couldn't eat it, no matter how many times I tried to convince myself it was no big deal.

"Why didn't you use fat-free cheese?" I was so upset my hand was shaking. "You have some in the fridge!"

"You girls need protein for your growing bones," Mom said. "A bit of cheese won't kill you."

That's what *she* thought. A bit of cheese would most definitely kill me.

"I'm not going to eat it." I crossed my arms over my chest. I knew Mom would get mad, but I couldn't stop myself. Every inch of my body was on high alert.

Danger! Abort!

"It's dinnertime, Riley." Mom sighed, a drawn-out "my life is so difficult" sigh. "You need to eat."

"I don't need to eat."

"Riley, cut the crap." My eyes widened. Mom *never* talked like that. Especially to me. I couldn't back down, though.

"I'll eat later. I'll eat salad." I pulled the big bowl toward me and scooped out some lettuce. *It's probably all* you're *going to eat, anyway.* (I didn't say that last part.)

"You'll eat more than lettuce, missy." Mom put a huge piece of lasagna on my plate. I stared at the gooey cheese. The delicious noodles. The homemade tomato sauce. My mouth literally watered. There was actual water in my mouth.

I wanted more than water in there. I wanted food. I wanted lasagna.

Except I couldn't have it. I wouldn't let myself. I pushed the plate away. *Pretend it's dog food*, I coached myself. *Pretend it's been poisoned. You don't want to eat poison.*

"Eat your food," Mom said. "This isn't all about you." She looked at the pile of bills on the other side of the table. Some were opened, some unopened. The pile was teetering, the top bill about to slide down the others like a toboggan on a blanket of freshly fallen snow. "I can't deal with this drama on top of everything else. Especially when your father has been working late all week."

I wanted to help Mom feel better. I knew that gymnastics costs a lot of money. I knew my parents were stressed. But they were stressing me out, too. Why couldn't Mom and Dad understand that I *couldn't* eat the lasagna?

Mom didn't push it. Julia ate her big piece of lasagna and Mom ate her teeny-tiny one. I ate my salad. Mom's hands trembled as she ate. She called the hospital the next day.

Back then, I thought Mom's hands were shaking with anger. Now I wonder if she was scared. If she felt as helpless then as I do now.

If Mom is just as human as me.

———

Aisha was upset after snack tonight. She didn't want to do a check-in with a counselor, so I got some paper from the craft cabinet. I asked her to draw with me.

Brenna came over to work on a collage. Aisha drew a house. She said it was the only thing she could draw well. I told her that was okay, that I wasn't that good, either. Everyone else wandered over, too. They watched and we talked as I tried to draw Meredith.

We all started talking, like how Emerson and Josie and I used to talk during sleepovers, when we were up for so long that we couldn't stop ourselves from sharing every single thing on our minds.

Brenna told us that two girls at school set up a whole website dedicated to why she's a total freak.

Laura told us she's afraid her boyfriend hasn't kissed her yet because she's not skinny enough.

Aisha told us her parents won't let her celebrate Ramadan this year, that that's "one whole month of starving I'll miss out on."

I wanted to tell them about Talia making fun of me. I opened my mouth a few times, the confession dancing on the tip of my tongue. I didn't, though. It may have felt like a sleepover, but I knew it wasn't. If I told them how I used to be bigger, they might make fun of me. They might see me differently.

But maybe they *would* understand. Maybe they're *not* staring at my body, separating it into pieces that need to be whittled down to fit. After all, everyone here has problems. We're all worried about something. And tonight, their compliments weren't about my body.

The other girls watched as I drew Meredith. No one told me

her ears were too pointy. No one said my shadowing wasn't good enough.

I was the only one doing that.

Meredith told me I was talented and that she would keep the picture forever. "I look . . . pretty," she said. She sounded like she'd discovered buried treasure.

Laura told me it was cool how I got us all to hang out together.

Aisha told me I made her feel better.

I think they like me.

DAY ELEVEN: THURSDAY

I didn't do crunches last night. Ali didn't either. The night staff kept looking in at us after lights-out, so we never got a chance. I wonder if they suspect anything. I wonder if we're going to get in trouble. I wonder if I should stop for good.

Ali's upset. She keeps glaring at me like it's my fault she didn't get to exercise.

"Did you tell anyone?"

I was so surprised that I practically yelled the word *no*. I probably sounded super guilty, because Ali stepped closer. She peered into my eyes. "Are you telling the truth?"

My armpits started to sweat, like they do when I have to give a book report in front of the class. (*Totally* the most embarrassing thing ever. At least I know to wear black on presentation days now.) "I didn't say anything."

"I hope not. Because I feel gross this morning."

Maybe Ali feels gross, but I feel . . . good? If not good, then not bad. Not guilty.

I feel like I'm doing the right thing.

"I'm hungry." The second I said it, I wished I could stuff the words back in my mouth. Stuff them in like the food I stuff in every day.

I'm more stuffed than a teddy bear.

If I'm eating more than ever, why am I hungry, though? I think that's why I told Willow. I wanted an answer. I wanted confirmation that my body wasn't broken, that I hadn't hurt it beyond repair.

"Of course you're hungry." Willow smiled, but it wasn't a know-it-all, "look how smart I am" smile. It was the kind of smile Mom used to give me when I was afraid of monsters underneath my bed. When she mixed rose petals with water in a spray bottle and labeled it MONSTER SPRAY. When we were united against a common enemy.

"You've been starving your body for a while now," Willow said. "So even though your brain might feel like you're eating a lot, your *body* is screaming that it wants more. That it *needs* more." Willow adjusted her headband. She wears the coolest headbands. Yesterday's was gold with sparkly stars. Today's was a long paisley scarf she knotted at her neck. The ends trailed down her back like long floppy ears. "You have a big deficit to make up for. *Plus*, your metabolism is finally working again."

"But I don't like being hungry. I don't want to eat more."

The sick part of me doesn't want more food. That part knows that more food means gaining weight faster.

The healthy part of me likes eating, though. It likes laughing. It likes living in a world without fuzz around the edges.

"So it's okay if I eat more?" I wasn't sure if I was asking Willow for permission or telling myself that it was okay to want. I just knew that I had to say the words out loud. I had to hear her answer.

"It's okay," Willow said. "It's normal. Your body is doing exactly what it's supposed to be doing. It's repairing. It's learning to trust you. It's getting strong so you can live your life."

I'm still not sure how I feel about that word: *strong*. It *sounds* like a good word. It makes me feel powerful. Determined. Like a superhero.

But it also makes me sound big. Superheroes have muscles. Superheroes weigh more.

But who really cares about Wonder Woman's weight, as long as she saves the world?

———

I just farted three times in a row, and the room smells like death. I really hope no one notices, but Ali keeps looking at me. She's rifling through an old copy of O magazine for art therapy, cutting out phrases like "Live Your Best Life" and "The Power of You" for the collages we're making.

I wonder if she'll start blackmailing me because of my death farts, too.

It probably wouldn't be a big deal if I admitted it was me. That's something Willow told me, that farting is normal while our bodies are getting used to food again. Constipation, too. And bloating. So basically our stomachs are plotting revenge against us.

"You're all farting machines now." Willow laughed. I did, too. (Farts never stop being funny.) "But it'll level off, just like your anxiety. That's what you have to remember when you're eating and when your stomach hurts. Anxiety comes in waves. It starts out low, then peaks into panic."

I nodded. I know that feeling. My anxiety peaks all the time. Especially when I eat fear foods. We talked about fear foods during Nutrition Group yesterday.

Brenna's is ice cream.

Laura's are juice and butter.

Meredith's is chocolate.

Mine is peanut butter.

Normal people are afraid of undercooked meat. Or raw eggs. Stuff that can make them sick. For us, fear foods are things we're afraid will make us gain weight or lose control. In here, they make us try new things to prove our fear foods won't kill us.

"Remember, if you wait out the anxiety and surf the wave . . ." Willow pretended she was on a surfboard. "Then the anxiety will crest and fall. You'll realize there's nothing to be afraid of. Whether it's a peanut butter sandwich or adjusting to a new body shape, everything becomes normal after a little while, especially now that you're feeding your brain enough to reason with it." She pretended to fall off her surfboard. I rolled my eyes.

What Willow said made sense. She made me want to believe her. She made me want to eat a peanut butter sandwich. I really do like peanut butter. Once I even dreamed about it. (Okay, twice.)

That's why I let Willow convince me to put it on my menu for tomorrow.

"I know you can do this, Riley. I promise that once you have that sandwich, you'll realize peanut butter isn't such a big deal. That it's normal to fuel your body." She looked me in the eye. "Do you trust me?"

Ed told me not to trust her. He told me Willow was a big lying liar who lies. He said I'd die if I ate that sandwich.

"I trust you," I told her. "I can do it."

I still don't know if I can. But I'm going to try.

I'm going to fart, too, apparently.

———

I feel like this place is a time capsule, sealed up and preserved for millions of years. When I get out, the ice caps will be melted. Elephants will be extinct and the plants will have mutated into eight-foot-tall beanstalks. Everyone I know and love will be gone.

It's a scary thought.

It's also a nice thought. Because if everyone I know is gone, no one will know me as Skinny Riley.

I can be whoever I want to be.

DAY TWELVE: FRIDAY

I ate the sandwich!

I feel proud but also really freaked out. Brenna said I'm awesome and gave me a big hug. She had cake for her lunch dessert, which still makes *her* nervous. We gave each other pep talks before we went into the dining room. We were like eating disorder cheerleaders but without the pleated skirts and pom-poms.

She rocked it. I rocked it.

We did it.

Wow.

———

Emerson came to visit tonight! I didn't know she was coming, so it was a total surprise. I was sitting in the group room before evening snack, trying to decide between watching boring *Wheel of Fortune* or *Star Wars: The Last Jedi*. Jean poked her head in the door.

"You have a visitor, Riley!"

Mom? I didn't know she was coming. I thought she had an exhibition tonight. I felt like dogs do when they spot a squirrel in the corner of their eye. I whipped my head around so fast my ponytail turned into a real tail.

Wag wag! Squirrel!

No Mom.

But seeing Emerson was almost as awesome!

She ran over but stopped about a foot away. "Are we allowed to hug?" She peeked at Jean. "Is that against the rules?"

I laughed. An "I haven't laughed with you in months" laugh. A "you're here and you didn't forget about me" laugh. I'd forgotten what it felt like to be happy. To see Emerson and not have my first thought be about how I can hide my eating stuff from her.

I forgot about the peanut butter. I forgot about Ali. At that moment, it was just me and Emerson. I was "in the moment," like they teach us in Mindfulness Group. I didn't worry about the past and I didn't worry about the future. I was just glad to see my friend.

It's like there's been this veil between us for the past year and someone finally lifted it up. Maybe *I* lifted it up.

Is this what they mean when they say that recovery is worth it? That I can *keep* feeling moments of happiness like this? I felt sparkly, like I could dash through a field of rainbows or ride on the back of a unicorn.

Emerson was here! She looked the same, too. The same curly red hair poofing out around her face. The same green eyes, so much like mine but somehow way prettier. Even though she looked like she'd come right from her track meet, with her hair pulled back and her dirty Asics still on, my happiness to see Emerson outweighed my jealousy that she got to run today and I didn't.

We hugged, but she pulled back right away like I was contagious. Like I was in the "sick" part of the hospital instead of the mental wing. I tried not to take it personally. Willow's been working with me on not automatically assuming people think badly of me.

Before we left to go to my room, Jean asked Emerson if she had any "contraband."

"Like weapons?" Emerson's eyes were wide.

I shook my head. "Like food, silly. Or sharps."

"Sharps?"

"Stuff like scissors," I explained.

"Why?"

"So people can't hurt themselves." I said it matter-of-factly, but Emerson looked like she'd found out the Tooth Fairy isn't real.

"Patients here hurt themselves?" Emerson asked. "That's so scary."

"It is, but it's just a problem they're dealing with. They're getting help, like me."

That's when I realized something. That twelve days on an eating disorder unit is enough time to start thinking in a new way. To realize that even though the rest of the world may think of us as sick, we're all just people with our own issues.

We're all trying to get better in our own ways.

That's not scary, that's *amazing*.

It made me think about Julia, too. How she works to get better at gymnastics with her coaches and sometimes even Mom yelling at her and correcting her. How she gets bumps and bruises on the outside, just like I'm getting them on the inside.

How everyone outside of the hospital probably has their own problems. (Except Talia. I bet Talia's only problem is a thunderstorm when she's wearing a full face of makeup. Even then, I bet she wears all waterproof stuff.)

After a while, though, it started to seem like Emerson had a problem, too—a problem with being at the hospital. When Jean searched her backpack and took her gum away, Emerson squirmed. When I talked about my meal plan and how I freaked out about peanut butter, she didn't listen. Emerson kept peeking out the door, like she was waiting for a horde of zombies to walk by. And when I asked Emerson about school, she basically avoided my questions. Here's what I found out:

Track: "It's good. We won today."

School: "It's hard. Mrs. Monahan gave two pop quizzes last week."

Josie: "I'm not sure. You'll have to ask her."

Emerson didn't ask me any questions and she barely

answered mine, even when I brought up the art class she'd seemed so excited about.

"It sounds so fun!"

Emerson looked at her fingernails, which were teal and gold and shimmered like a mermaid's tail. Mine were bare and jagged because I've been biting them since I got here.

"Are you sure you'll be out by then?" she asked. "And, you know, okay to do stuff? I know Coach Jackson said you won't be ready for regionals. Can you still do art?"

"Coach said *what*?" I gripped my hands into fists. "Of *course* I'll be out in time to qualify for regionals. What, do you think I'm too huge and slow now?"

I don't know why I was so defensive. Why regionals suddenly mattered so much to me. I mean, yeah, I've had urges to run in here. But that's different from wanting to do *track*. I haven't thought about racing much at all, actually. The idea of competing makes me exhausted.

"No!" Emerson waved her hands in the air. "I didn't say that. It's just, uh, what I heard. Plus, your mom told my mom you didn't know when you'd be getting out."

"Soon. I'll be out soon. *And* I'll be faster than ever." I glared at Emerson. "Plus, of course I can still *draw*. Anorexia didn't break my hands."

Emerson flinched at the word *anorexia*. I used to do that, too, before I got in here. Now it's normal to throw out words like *bulimia* and *binge, anorexia* and *purge*. They're just words. Labels that don't say anything about who we are.

(That's what the counselors tell us, at least. That's what I'm trying to believe.)

"Maybe we should wait to sign up," Emerson said. "Just in case."

In case of what? I wanted to yell. *In case you don't want to be friends with me if I'm not Runner Riley anymore? In case Coach really does decide I can't run?*

All of a sudden Emerson was like a stranger. Like the veil hadn't lifted after all but turned into a brick wall instead.

I don't feel sparkly anymore.

DAY THIRTEEN: SATURDAY

Mom visited.

Dad didn't visit.

I asked Mom about what Emerson had said. Mom said Emerson was right, that Coach Jackson isn't letting me run in any of the qualifying meets for regionals even *if* I'm discharged in time. He says it's a matter of "responsibility" and "health." That I need to be 100 percent before I run again. That he could be blamed if I get hurt.

I hate that I won't be able to run anytime soon. I also hate that deep down, I'm relieved. I hate that I'm so tired, inside and out.

I should *want* to run. I should be visualizing the starting blocks in my head, seeing my arms pump and my legs whirl. I should be ready to slip into my uniform and cleats the second I march out the hospital door.

Should, should, should.

I don't want to think like this. I have to be a runner. I *am* a runner.

I've lost so much in here. I can't give up that part of myself, too.

I *want* to give up that part of myself, though. I want to draw.

Maybe I'll find something else I love even more than drawing.

My head keeps yelling at me.

My heart keeps yelling at me.

My heart is louder today.

Maybe I don't have to be a runner to be me.

DAY FIFTEEN: MONDAY

Another day, another weight check, another cup of Gatorade.

Another shower, too. The counselors make us keep the doors open while we shower, so we don't throw up or do jumping jacks or whatever. Slippery jumping jacks would be totally dangerous. I bet Ali has done them, though. She did crunches again last night.

I didn't. It was the first time I resisted the urge. My head kept yelling at me to give in: *Do them do them do them.*

Right now it's yelling at me again: *Why didn't you do crunches? You can't run anymore. You don't even want to run anymore. Let this be your exercise!*

> **Ed:** *You're gross. You've been eating so much. You're going to get huge.*
>
> **Healthy Voice:** *It's okay to be bigger. I'm getting happier, too.*
>
> **Ed:** *No. You have to fix yourself. Don't eat. Do crunches tonight. You'll feel better.*

Healthy Voice: *But I'm not supposed to. I'm proud that I'm trying to recover.*

Ed: *You're weak. You're not Skinny Riley anymore.*

Healthy Voice: *Not exercising makes me strong.*
A different kind of strong.

I hate that voice. I want to stick some duct tape over its lips. Duct tape is awesome. You can make wallets out of that stuff. Purses, too. Some girl online made a prom dress. Duct tape is way strong, too. I bet if you taped a bunch of strips together, it could hold up a whole person. A small person, anyway. Like the person I don't have to be anymore.

I did a check-in today. It was the first one I've sought out all on my own. I told Heather that I felt like running. I told her that I *didn't* feel like running at the same time. That I was relieved I didn't have to try to make regionals and confused about *being* relieved.

"My body feels gross." I looked at the ground while I talked to her. It felt weird talking to someone besides Willow about my problems. I thought Heather was going to tell me I was silly for worrying. I needed to talk to *someone*, though, and Brenna said that check-ins help her.

"For the first time ever, I don't have the energy to 'fix' myself. I don't *want* to fix myself. But then five seconds later all I want is to go back in time to when I was super sick. Is that normal? Am I broken?"

Heather shook her head. She told me that recovery isn't a straight line and that it's normal to shift between "Yay, recovery!" and "Everything is awful" in the same day.

"In the same minute even," she reassured me. "You can have ups and downs, as long as you stay on the path. The line doesn't have to be straight, as long as you keep moving forward and keep trying.

"Right now, you can't help thinking this way," Heather said. "It just happens. Your brain goes there. But we're training your brain *not* to go there. We're teaching you to fight back."

I like the idea of brain training. It makes me think of Xavier Academy, the school where the X-Men go to learn to control their powers. To do good instead of evil. (Brenna loaned me one of those comics yesterday. She's trying to teach me to be a better geek. She says I'm getting an A-plus so far.)

This is my Academy, where I can learn how to stop thinking about the butter on my toast this morning. Where I can learn to stop analyzing every millimeter of my body.

"Thoughts aren't actions," Heather said. "And you're not *doing* anything wrong."

That's where she's wrong, though. Because I *am* doing something wrong. Actually, I'm *not* doing something. I'm not telling anyone about Ali. I'm worried about her. She keeps having to drink Boosts, *and* she's yelling at the counselors a lot.

I used to be jealous of Ali, but now I see her differently: She has dark circles under her eyes. She never smiles.

Last night Ali gasped for breath a bunch of times. I thought she was going to die. I almost got up and went to the nurses' station for help, but then she stopped. What if something *does* happen? It'll be all my fault. I have to tell someone.

DAY SIXTEEN: TUESDAY

Today's Willow's birthday. I don't know how Meredith found out, but she did. We're having a meeting in the group room this afternoon to plan a party!

Meredith told us the news in a whisper, like she was a superspy. A secret ballerina superspy.

"Message received," I whispered back. "Agent Logan, over and out." Meredith started to giggle, but I put my finger to my lips. "Silence is priority number one," I whispered. "Super-stealth mode is activated. Agent Logan will be incommunicado until our next rendezvous point." I stuck out my hand for a secret handshake. Only it turns out you really can't do a secret handshake if the other person has no idea what you're doing. So I basically flailed my hand in the air and slapped Meredith's palm. That's when Heather came out with her clipboard. She gave me the weirdest look ever.

"Over and out," I mumbled.

The other girls broke into giggles. Heather rolled her eyes. That made us laugh more.

Willow's turning thirty. I thought she was younger, but

Meredith overheard Willow say her age. Thirty is a big birthday. When Aunt Rose turned thirty, she quit her teaching job and went to Italy for three months. She came back engaged to a guy from her bike tour named Raoul, who lived with her in Boston for a while and then moved to California to be a yogi. Aunt Rose cried for two weeks and then decided she still wanted to be a teacher after all.

Aunt Rose has a very complicated life.

My whole point is that thirty is a big birthday, one where you stop and think about what you want.

We all like Willow. That's why we decided that we don't want her to quit her job and move to Italy. We want her to stay here and keep helping girls like us.

"We have to throw her a birthday party." Meredith bounced up and down on the toes of her flats. They're the closest she can get to ballet slippers in here. "Maybe they'll even let us dance."

"Ooooh, yes!" Brenna bounced in her seat. Today is a very bouncy day. "We can put up balloons and streamers and sing 'Happy Birthday' and get her presents and have cake!"

"Extra cake?" Laura asked. "On top of our meal plan? No way."

She had a point. "Maybe we can have cake as *part* of our meal plan?" Brenna asked.

"Of course you want cake," Ali mumbled. We all still heard her being a jerk, though.

"Don't say stuff like that." *I* didn't mumble. Brenna doesn't deserve snarky comments about what she eats. None of us deserve snarky comments about what we eat.

"Stuff like what?" Ali asked. "I can say whatever I want." She raised an eyebrow at me. "Like stuff certain people are doing at night."

"No one's doing anything at night except sleeping, Ali." Aisha butted in, then turned her back on Ali. So did Meredith. So did everyone else. They didn't ask what Ali was talking about. They just took my side. They took Brenna's side. And we kept planning the party.

It wasn't like at school, when whatever Talia says becomes law. When the girls she hates become the girls *everyone* hates. Today everyone had a mind of her own.

And they picked me.

(We're still deciding about the cake.)

———

We didn't have streamers, so we made those paper chains Julia and I used to decorate the Christmas tree with, where you tape construction paper strips into circles and hook them into a long strand. Instead of red and green, we used every color of the rainbow.

Instead of balloons, we made signs:

Happy Birthday, Willow!

Thank you for helping us!

You're a great therapist!

I overheard Heather and Jean talking about how mature we were. They also made up some fake meeting for Willow to go to while we decorated. When Willow finally came in, she was so surprised she shrieked. "Oh my goodness, girls! You are the sweetest people ever. I'll never forget this day."

We played music! (Even some non-approved music with "questionable lyrics.")

We danced! (For about five minutes, until Jean told us we were being too active.)

It was so much fun.

———

Laura's going out to dinner with her parents tonight. She got a special pass since her dad is going overseas this weekend. He's in the army and is going back to Afghanistan. Laura looked upset when she told us in group, so I tried to talk to her after. She totally shut me out, which made me think of Josie.

I don't know what I can do to make things up to her. I wish I had a time machine, so I could go back and throw her the biggest, bestest birthday party ever. I'd get a karaoke machine, because Josie loves them, and we'd sing "Love Is an Open Door," even though karaoke is the most embarrassing thing ever.

I'd even go out to eat for her, like Laura's doing. (Her family is going to Frankie J's, a super-scary Italian restaurant whose portions are as big as my head. Maybe bigger.)

"What does a big plate of pasta feel like to *you*?" Willow asked me in our session.

"Like I'm on a roller coaster," I answered. "Like my stomach is dropping out of my body and the whole world is falling away." I thought for another minute. I like metaphors. So does Mrs. Monahan. She'd be proud of me. "You know how there's no gravity in space?"

Willow nodded, all therapist-like. She just needed a sweater with elbow patches on it. Or a pipe. Except those are gross.

"You know how whenever astronauts are floating in space, they're tethered by a cord? A really strong one, so it doesn't break and send them into the void forever? When I think about eating at Frankie J's, it's like I'm in outer space. But instead of a cord, there's an elastic band. One of those really thin ones that break all the time, like on cheap Halloween masks."

I was sure Willow was going to laugh at my metaphor. I stared at her carpet. It's dark red with yellow dots, like bits of gold are embedded in there.

"Keep going," she prompted.

"If I eat something scary, that band will snap. I'll be in space." I whispered the last part.

"What's so scary about outer space?"

I raised my eyebrows at her. "It's outer space. Duh. You keep floating forever and ever and you can never get back home and then you *die*."

"But what if you *don't* die?"

"That's a silly question," I said. "Of course you die. You can't survive in outer space. It's dark and bleak and there's no one else around. There's no food."

Willow raised her eyebrow at the word *food*. She didn't say anything, though. I bet there's a special class in shrink school called How to Be Quiet to Best Unnerve Your Patients. I bet Willow aced that class.

"But what if you *don't* die?" she asked again. "What if outer space *isn't* dark and scary? What if it's just that no one you know has reported back after their elastic snapped?"

I looked up from the carpet.

"What if it's beautiful in space?" Willow asked. "Full of supernovas and exploding stars and brilliant colors? What if it's the most wonderful place in the world, but you're too scared to release your tether and find out?"

I wanted to ask her what colors were out there and how bright they were. But all I could feel was the elastic band snapping and sending me hurtling into the darkness.

"What if it *is* dark and cold, though?"

"Isn't it like that now?" Willow asked. "So why not try for a supernova? You have nothing to lose."

DAY SEVENTEEN: WEDNESDAY

Ali did crunches again last night.

Ali sounded like she was dying again.

I have to do something.

———

I told Willow about the crunches. I told her about me and I told her about Ali. I almost chickened out. I felt like I was going to faint. But I did it.

Willow told me she was proud of me for admitting what I'd done and asking for help.

She said that this, more than anything, told her I was on the "road to recovery."

"You didn't have to tell me anything," Willow said. "You could have kept it a secret, hid it in the shadows where it would grow to be more fierce and dangerous." Willow was smiling so big I bet it hurt her jaw. "You know what you are, Riley?"

"What?"

"You're a superhero. And you're saving yourself."

I thought of all the comic books Brenna reads and all the kick-butt heroines in them. I imagined myself in a cape, my feet planted on the ground, my fist raised to the sky.

Superheroes aren't weak. Neither am I.

"Is Ali going to get in trouble?" My voice was shaking. "Because that's something superheroes probably don't do. They don't betray their friends or break promises."

"Real friends break promises when it's important. Especially when someone's life is on the line. You're *helping* Ali by telling me," Willow said. "That's *my* promise to you."

DAY EIGHTEEN: THURSDAY

They switched Ali's room last night. The counselors told us she was moving across the hall and wouldn't answer *any* of our questions. I know they've confronted her, though, because they have a staff member checking her room every fifteen minutes at night.

Ali hates me. She keeps looking at me like I'm a slab of steak and she's a hungry tiger.

Even dealing with Talia would be better than this. At least outside of the hospital I'd be doing other stuff besides eating. In here, that's all there is: food and emotions and crying.

The world is going on without me.

I think my drawing is getting better, at least. I've been doing it all the time, in *and* out of art therapy. I've drawn all the girls in here. I've drawn them all more than once, actually, in different poses and in different lighting. Mom was right, too. I was bad at shadowing. That's why my noses always looked strange. But now that I've drawn and redrawn and experimented, I'm getting better at it.

I'm not a failure. I'm a work in progress.

Maybe I can work hard and take that class with Emerson and then take *more* classes and get better and better and someday become a professional artist. How cool would that be? I don't have to display in Mom's gallery, either. There are tons of other galleries and tons of other paths to take. I just have to find *my* path.

I can't be an artist with an eating disorder, though. Art is all about trying new things, exploring the world and capturing those emotions. I don't *have* emotions when I'm sick. I'm too scared to explore anything when I'm focused on my body.

I need to be free to live my life.

I can't control my body and be an artist. I can't control my body and be *me*.

Mom and Julia came to visit tonight. Mom tried to convince me to ask for a pass—she wanted us to go out to eat together—but there's no way I'm ready for that yet.

"You're doing so well!" she said.

I'm not doing *that* well, though. The idea of Mom staring at me while I stare at a menu makes my heart race faster than it does when I run the 400 meter. What if I order more food than they usually have me eat in here? What if the salad comes with dressing already on it? What if Mom pressures me to order dessert and it's delicious and I eat and eat until it's gone? I won't be able to run to burn off the calories, and if I throw a fit or get anxious, Mom will be disappointed.

Julia brought a bunch of board games instead. We played

Settlers of Catan and Ticket to Ride and King of Tokyo. King of Tokyo is boring with three players, so Brenna and Laura joined us. Brenna got so into it she started jumping up and down and pretending to be Godzilla whenever it was her turn. It was so funny. At first Laura acted embarrassed by us, but I could tell she had fun, too. Her boyfriend hasn't been visiting or returning her e-mails, so she's been a super grump lately.

I get that. It's lonely in here.

It's like that lost city of Atlantis, the one that sank into the ocean, never to be seen again. Some explorers think it's a real thing and spend their entire careers searching for the gleaming towers beneath the surface. Most people think it's a myth, though. If Atlantis *was* real, the world has forgotten it ever existed. Everyone else has gone on with their lives. Made new friends. Moved on.

Meanwhile all of us underwater people are struggling to swim up to the surface. *Here I am! Find me! See me!*

At least Julia is still searching for Atlantis. She didn't talk about my body at all—unlike Mom, who kept examining me like she was a human X-ray machine. Julia talked about TV instead. Apparently this new show premiered last night that everyone in her class is "totally obsessed with." She told me about the main character and his magic powers and the boy he likes and the girl who likes him and how "the scene with the shapeshifter was soooooooooo cool."

I listened the whole time and didn't even laugh at all the funny faces Julia was making. I bet I earned major big-sister points for that. Not like the negative seven million points I've earned in the past year, when I never said congratulations after a good meet and never had time to help Julia with her homework. After a while, Julia started tiptoeing around me like I was a bomb about to erupt. She didn't ask me to do anything with her.

Julia was too busy growing her awesome life.

I was too busy shrinking mine.

Today was different, though. Today we acted like sisters. Julia didn't talk about gymnastics. I didn't talk about food. She treated Brenna and Laura like normal people, too, not circus freaks.

At the end of their visit, Mom sent Julia into the hallway to wait for her. After she left, Mom put her arm around me. I snuggled into her side. Half of me was afraid she was going to jump away like Emerson did or start chiding me for being too thin. The other half was glad to have my mom here.

I pretend I'm not scared, but I really am. I'm scared a lot. I just want everyone to *think* I'm strong.

"Are you mad at me?" I asked.

"Riley!" Mom looked so shocked that I thought she *was* mad at me. I thought she was going to yell. Or even worse, say how disappointed she was that I'm not all the way better yet.

She didn't.

"Honey, I'm not even the smallest bit mad at you." Mom tilted my chin up so I was looking into her eyes. It's what she does when I'm in trouble and she wants me to make eye contact. That's why I didn't believe her.

"You're not lying?"

"I wouldn't lie to you," Mom said. "I promise."

"But *I* lied to *you*." I felt the tears welling up. I didn't want to cry. I couldn't be weak. I had to show Mom I was strong. "I lied and I snuck around."

"You did," Mom said. "You made some mistakes, like all kids do."

"Julia doesn't make mistakes," I mumbled.

Mom laughed. "Oh, yes, she does. Julia talks back and messes up her room and—"

"And messes up her vault? That's what I heard you say last month. That she's not working hard enough."

"Oh, Riley." Mom pulled away and took a deep breath, then hugged me again. "I don't care about Julia's vault. Or Julia's scores. Or your weight."

"You care about *your* weight," I said. "And you talk about gymnastics *all the time*." I wanted to say something about my art, but I couldn't get there quite yet. It would hurt too much if Mom confirmed that she judged my talent. I'd be too nervous if she asked to see what I'm working on. I'll save that talk for later.

"I do watch my weight," Mom said. "I diet sometimes. But that's me, not you. We're different people. You have to remember that."

Of course I know we're different people. Mom's forty-two and I'm twelve. Mom has gray hair and I have pimples. She likes boring documentaries and I like action movies.

That doesn't mean I'm okay with her dieting, though.

This is the kind of stuff we talk about in Assertiveness Group: Speaking up when we want something from a family member. Putting our needs into words. Heather worked on it with us yesterday:

Brenna practiced asking her sister to stop making fun of her.

Meredith practiced telling her dad that ballerinas are athletes, too.

I practiced telling Mom and Dad that I wanted them to pay more attention to me.

I rehearsed looking them in the eye and making my voice firm but not loud.

I rehearsed sitting up straight and squaring my shoulders.

I did none of those things today.

I didn't tell Mom that *her* diets make *me* want to diet. I didn't tell Mom that when *she* talks about losing weight, *I* want to lose weight. That even though I *know* weight loss isn't a competition, I always *feel* like it is. I always want to win.

"Okay," I said instead. "I'll remember that."

"Good." Mom's phone buzzed. Her fingers tapped away. "Hold on, it's your father."

"Can I talk to him?"

"One sec." More tapping. "Sorry, honey, he had to go. He sends his love, though."

"Why can't he tell me himself?" It would take *one minute* of his day. Twenty seconds even.

"He has a meeting, I think."

I'm more important than a meeting. But I didn't say that to Mom. I wanted her to go home. I wanted to be alone.

"Mom?"

"Yes?"

"I love you." I couldn't say anything else, but I could say that. Maybe someday I'll learn to say more.

"I love you, too, honey. You're doing so well. You look healthier."

My heart stopped. I literally felt it stop. For one heartbeat of a moment I ceased to exist. I hovered outside myself, hearing Mom's words as my body went numb.

Healthy.

Does that word mean the same thing to me anymore? Does it mean that I'm not special? That I'm weak? Or does it mean that I'm . . . healthy?

Full of health.

Not about to die.

The staff here doesn't talk about our bodies. They don't tell us we look "good" or "healthy" or "better." They talk about our personalities instead. Our smiles. Our talents.

"Brenna, I love how excited you were when you talked about your trip to the Wizarding World of Harry Potter!"

"Meredith, that story was hilarious."

"Aisha, I can tell you're a great friend."

"Laura, that insight was fantastic."

There's nothing to decode because we don't talk about weight. We talk about how we *feel* about weight, but not about how much we weigh. Mom doesn't know that rule, though. She doesn't know that she's pushed my brain into a whirlpool.

I tried to use my healthy voice. I tried to stop my thoughts before they turned into urges by picturing a big red STOP sign in my mind.

Being healthy is good. Being healthy means I'm not sick. It means I can take that art class with Emerson. It means I can go home.

But what if I go home and Mom's on a diet? What if I show her my newest drawings and she tells me they're awful? What if nothing changes but me? Will I be able to keep going, or will I slide back into sickness?

I don't want to be sick forever. I feel happier now. My body doesn't hurt as much. I can concentrate. I read three whole chapters in my book this afternoon without getting distracted. I can probably do schoolwork now.

I don't want to go back to where I was before.

DAY NINETEEN: FRIDAY

I ate ice cream and a hamburger at lunch today. I tried to do what Heather taught us in Mindfulness Group, to focus on the sensation of the food and how it tasted, but it was hard. I kept thinking about Ali and whether she's plotting her revenge. If she'll put poison into my food or get all the other girls to turn against me. If they'll hate me like Josie does.

Maybe that's what's always going to happen. People will be nice to me . . . until they realize what I'm really like. How boring and un-special I am. Then they'll abandon me. They'll find new friends and new things to do.

I kept thinking about Mom and how she refuses to stop dieting.

I kept thinking about everything wrong in my life. Then I felt guilty about feeling so angry. Compared to some people, I have small problems. I have a home. I have money to buy things. I'm not abused.

I still hurt, though.

I tried to think about how the ice cream was creamy and cold. How the mint was sharp on my tongue.

How the hamburger was juicy and the lettuce crunched in my mouth.

I didn't do a good job, even *without* Ali there to stare at me.

All I can think about is how I shouldn't have eaten them. How my body feels different. But body changes are okay, right? It's okay for my body to find where it's meant to be.

Right?

Ice cream and hamburgers are normal. Not freaking out about them is normal.

Right?

Willow says "normal" is eating when you're hungry and stopping when you're full. Eating what you want *when* you want it and listening to your body. It's eating too much sometimes because you really like oatmeal cookies. It's not eating a big breakfast because you're in a hurry but then making up for it with a bigger lunch. It's salad and French fries and broccoli and meat sauce. It's parties and treats and being honest.

But if *that's* normal, then the *world* isn't normal. Mom weighs herself all the time. Talia and Camille are always talking about their "thigh gaps." Even Josie tries to find the best angle for selfies so she doesn't look fat.

How can I eat "normally" when everyone else is doing the complete opposite? How can I eat a full meal for lunch while everyone around me is having a salad? I can't eat five times as much as everyone else. I just can't.

This all makes me so angry. The world won't change. My family won't change.

My face is hot and my breath is coming fast. The medication they put me on in here has been helping with my anxiety, but today I feel like someone lit a firecracker in my chest. It's sizzling and sparking and about to burst any second.

———

I checked my e-mail again. Emerson *still* hasn't written to apologize for acting weird. There was nothing from Josie, either. All I had was an e-mail from L.L.Bean, from when Mom used my e-mail to buy herself a new pair of slippers.

Even my junk mail isn't for me.

The more I think about Emerson, the madder I get. I'm not contagious. She doesn't need to tiptoe around the hospital like she's going to get chicken pox or break something. (Or break me.)

The more I think about *Josie*, the madder I get. Okay, fine, I skipped her birthday party. I lied. But she's done mean things, too. She let out the class hamster in fifth grade and blamed it on me.

The more I think about *Mom*, the madder I get. Why can't she stop dieting? I'm her daughter. Are a few pounds more important than me?

The more I think about *Dad*, the madder I get. I'm *his* daughter, too. Not a stranger or a character in a story he's reading, one he gets to close the book on whenever he's sick of her.

I'm even mad at Julia. Because she has something that lets her soar through the sky. She has something she's good at, something she loves.

I don't have anything.

Sizzle. Spark.

I know the way to get rid of this anxiety before it bursts into a Fourth of July celebration. I know how to feel better. I just can't do it in here.

———

Ali isn't talking to me. She ignores everything I say in group and pretends I'm not even in the room. This is worse than how Talia used to treat me at school. At least I knew how Talia felt about me. She told me. She told *everyone*.

With Ali, it's just silence. Cold silence. I bet she hates me.

Of course she hates me. All my friends hate me eventually.

———

I had meatloaf on my menu for dinner tonight. I've never had meatloaf before. Mom doesn't like it, so she's never made it.

"It's important to try new things," Willow said. "To form an opinion for yourself. Or even to change your opinion on things you've *convinced* yourself you don't like." She gave me that super-annoying look she's so good at. "I'm sure you don't know anything about that."

Willow is so obnoxious.

Here's my opinion: meatloaf is *gross*. It's mushy and tastes like wet dog food. And here's the worst part—even though I hated it, I *still* had to eat all of it. I couldn't even leave a crumb. Apparently that's considered "eating-disordered behavior."

"That's total crap."

I can't believe I actually said that out loud in the middle of the dining room! I never swear. And, okay, I know *crap* isn't *technically* a swear, but Tyler Holt gets in trouble for saying it in class all the time.

"Riley." Heather's voice was a warning. "Please don't speak like that in here. If you have a problem, you can address it after dinner in a check-in."

Ali smirked at me from across the table. I bet she was thinking I'd back down and be a Goody-Two-shoes.

"I don't want a check-in!"

I'm *not* a Goody-Two-shoes. And I'm not going to let these people run my life. I won't let Mom or Dad run my life, either. And if Emerson and Josie don't want to be my friends, *whatever*. I'll find better friends.

I'm tired of being ignored. I'm tired of being told what to do. I'm angry and I'm alone. I'm tired of working so hard at recovery and still feeling awful all the time.

Plus, it was the *principle* of the thing. No one should be forced to eat dog food. Especially when they're trying to teach us to *like* food.

"I think you *need* a check-in." Heather stared me down.

I stared back. "I'm not a kid! I don't need a time-out. What I need is for someone to listen to how unfair this is." *Sizzle spark!* I was tired of the slow burn. It was time for the bang.

"We can talk later." Heather looked at the stopwatch the counselors always have during meals. "Halfway through, girls. You have fifteen minutes left in lunch."

"We need to talk now!" I pushed my chair back and stood up, which is *totally* against the rules. I felt like Patrick Henry, that Revolutionary War patriot we read about in social studies, the one who shouted, "Give me liberty, or give me death!" I felt like a revolutionary. A revolutionary shouting about meatloaf, but still a revolutionary.

"Riley, do you need an emergency appointment with Willow? Do you need a Boost?" Heather looked at my almost-full plate.

"I don't need a Boost!" I exclaimed. "I need you to listen to me. I shouldn't have to finish my meatloaf. I don't like it."

"You still have to eat it. It's on your meal plan." Heather's voice sounded bored. I wondered if she'd had this same exact fight before. With Carah or Ivy, those phantom snowflake names.

"But why?" I pressed. "Because that's what 'normal eaters' do?"

"Well, yes." Heather didn't meet my eyes.

I pounced upon her uncertainty like a cat on a mouse. I told her that normal eaters *don't* finish meals sometimes. "Once Julia opened up a yogurt that had fuzzy mold on it and smelled disgusting. *She* didn't eat the yogurt. *She* threw it away."

"You're not Julia," Heather said.

No, I'm not. I'll never be Julia. I'll never be that naturally small. I'll never be that naturally good. Can't I have this *one thing*, then? Can't I just skip this *one meal*?

Nope.

"You still have to eat your meatloaf."

I looked at the other girls. I thought they'd stand up for me and we'd all charge out of the dining room together.

They kept eating, though. They stared at me with fascinated looks, like I was a circus act.

See the Amazing Bearded Woman in ring one!

The Muscled Lion Tamer in ring two!

The Enraged Meatloaf Girl in ring three! See her try not to cry!

"But I'm full," I said. "I don't want to eat."

"Rules are rules," Heather said. "You can't trust your body's fullness cues quite yet. It's still learning how to deal with a healthy amount of food. You have to give it time."

I didn't want to give it time.

I didn't want to eat wet dog food.

I didn't want to be "healthy." I didn't want to listen to Heather.

I don't want to listen to anyone.

It's my life. My choices.

"I'm not having the meatloaf." I raised my chin.

"Then you can have the Boost." Heather tapped her mani-cured fingers on the table, the ones that matched her pretty flowered skirt. I was wearing ratty old sweatpants with an elas-tic waist. "I'm surprised, Riley. This isn't like you."

Who is Heather to say what I'm like? Heather barely knows me. Heather doesn't know that my favorite book is *The Girl Who Drank the Moon*. She doesn't know that I'm the best tree climber in our whole neighborhood or that when I was little, my favorite food was broccoli dipped in ketchup. Heather knows what I weigh, and that's all that matters to her.

Maybe that's all that matters to anyone.

"I'm not going to have the Boost."

"Those are the rules, Riley." Heather said it so patiently, like she was speaking from a script, like I was a name on a chart instead of *Riley*, a girl with fears and feelings of her own.

"I don't care about the rules. I don't want to have the Boost."

I'm waiting for a check-in now. They're making me have one because I "caused trouble." Because they think I need to "process my feelings." Everyone just filed by on their way to the group room, peeking at me like I'm a tiger behind bars.

The staff does everything they can to stop us from analyzing our bodies like we're a science project, from making observations and testing hypotheses like we did before:

If I eat this much, then this will happen.

If I weigh this much, then my life will become like this.

They can't stop us from seeing ourselves, though. They can't stop us from seeing each other, our insides and our outsides. Right now, my insides feel just as ugly as my outsides.

It feels good to be ugly, though. It feels good to be mad, to forget about the pain of recovery and think about what everyone else is doing wrong instead.

Heather shouldn't have tried to make me eat that food.

Mom should listen to me.

Dad should see me.

I should be able to make my own decisions.

DAY TWENTY: SATURDAY

The second I woke up, the idea popped into my head: *Don't eat breakfast today.*

I knew it was Ed's voice, but he sounded so nice. His voice was sweet and caring, like Mom's when I don't feel good. When she rubs my back and gives me ginger ale and those crackers that only taste good when I'm sick.

Not eating made you feel better yesterday. It made you forget.

Remember how restricting made you feel? You can feel like that again if you listen to me.

Last year, Camille had a hypnotist at her birthday party. At first, Emerson and Josie and I made fun of the whole thing. *Obviously* hypnotists are fake. There's no way we'd let someone take control of *our* bodies.

Then Madame Rosita picked Emerson to go onstage. (Camille's parents rented a stage, of course. *And* a karaoke machine. I think that's why she invited us; to show off all her money.) This was after the hypnotist made Luca quack like a chicken and Jarrett burp the alphabet. Madame Rosita did the classic "dangling a necklace in front of Emerson's face while muttering chants" thing, and all of a sudden, Emerson started singing at the top of her lungs. First "Yankee Doodle Dandy." Then "When the Saints Go Marching In" and "John Jacob Jingleheimer Schmidt." Emerson does *not* sing, either. She's almost as bad as me. But that day she sang. She couldn't resist.

That's what Ed is like. He chants magic spells and incantations, ones I have to obey.

I'm too tired to resist anymore. I don't want to fight Ed, especially if no one's going to fight *with* me.

So I won't. I may not recover, but at least I'll weigh less.

I feel skinnier. My stomach feels lighter.

I feel like I can fly.

—

I didn't eat breakfast. I had a Boost drink instead.

I've been eating so much in here that I've forgotten what it's like to be hungry.

It doesn't feel as good as I remember.

—

Brenna's been quiet all day. She didn't eat breakfast, either. Well, she ate one bite of toast. But then she crossed her arms over her chest and stared at Gabi like she was doing one of those "save the trees" sit-ins.

She didn't drink the Boost, either, which was weird. Brenna doesn't do stuff like that.

I usually don't, either.

I asked her if she was okay after movement class. We do "gentle" yoga here once a week, which is basically stretching. It's all the exercise they let us do. (Yoga is so not my thing, which is why I haven't written about it yet. I'm not bendy at *all*. Meredith is basically Silly Putty in human form.)

"I'm not okay. I shouldn't be eating anyway." Then Brenna ran out of the room. I didn't know what to do. A good friend would run after her. A good friend would hug her and tell her everything is going to be okay.

I don't want to be a good friend today, though. And everything might *not* be okay. I don't even know what to say to make *myself* feel better. How can I help anybody else?

It's hard to see Brenna not eat. I want Brenna to recover. I want *all* these girls to recover. Even Ali. (Maybe then she wouldn't be so mean. Maybe then I wouldn't have to avoid her like I used to avoid Talia.) They deserve a life without an eating disorder. They're all already perfect.

I wish I could help Brenna realize that even if she *is* big, she deserves food. Deep down, I know I deserve food, too. I know I'm doing the wrong thing by pushing it away.

But right now, it feels good to be bad.

———

Still no e-mail from Emerson.

Nothing from Josie.

Mom and Dad are at Julia's gymnastics meet today, where they'll sweep her up in a hug after she wins ribbons and medals and probably a trip to Disney World.

Brenna's been quiet all morning.

I've been drawing all morning. Aisha tried to sit with me, but I told her I wanted to be alone. I don't want to talk. I don't want to listen.

I want to be sad.

I tried to draw myself again. They won't let me use a mirror for reference, so I'm going on memory. I drew an oval for my face, and big eyes. I gave myself a mouth with a full lower lip and a non-existent upper one, then slightly rounded cheeks. Shoulder-length hair and a narrow nose.

My drawing looked like a stranger.

The cheeks were too puffy, so I erased them.

The hair was too scraggly, so I erased it.

I drew and erased until the paper ripped. Until my image was as smudged and mangled as I feel.

———

It's Saturday. When I was a kid, Dad and I used to wake up early and go to Dunkin' Donuts every Saturday morning. Dad would get a jelly doughnut and I'd get ten Munchkins: five glazed and five chocolate. Every week, Dad told me I could eat half of them now and half later, but he always caved and let me eat all ten. Then we went to the toy store in the center of town. We both smelled like coffee after sitting in Dunks, and we both played with the train table for hours. It was our special time. I had Saturdays and Julia had Sundays.

Now Dad's afraid of me.

And I have nothing.

———

I usually don't go back to my room after lunch. I troop into the group room with everyone else and we sit together and journal as we digest.

I ate all my lunch today. Part of me wanted to skip another meal, but I was too hungry to rebel. I guess I was too hungry to be careful, too, because I spilled ketchup on my hoodie and had to get a clean one from my room. (I have five hoodies here now. Hoodies are a top priority.)

I thought my room would be empty, but Jean was there. She was bent over, her scrub-covered butt sticking into the air, her hand shoved underneath my mattress.

"What are you doing?" I shrieked. "Do you have a warrant to search my stuff?" We learned about searches and seizures at school this year. That's when the police go into your house and look through everything. They can only do that if they have proof you've committed a crime. Which Jean definitely did not.

These people aren't the police, either, so it's *extra* illegal to search my stuff.

Jean dug deeper under the mattress. "Aha!"

"Aha what?" I don't keep anything under my bed, not even my journal. I'm not *that* dumb. I *used* to keep it there at home, but then Julia found it in third grade and read all about how I wanted to be a famous singer. She made fun of me for *weeks* because I sound like a frog with a sore throat when I try to sing in tune.

"You need a reason to search through my stuff," I said. "It's the law."

"*This* isn't a reason?" Jean held out her hand. There was a smooshed brown blob there. I stepped closer. It was a crushed brownie. I had a brownie at dinner yesterday. Why was there a brownie under my mattress? The two words floated through my head:

Brownie.

Mattress.

Brownie.

Mattress.

The ideas never connected, though, like a Venn diagram that refused to overlap. My mind couldn't make sense of what was going on—until Jean told me what *she* thought was going on.

"You hid food in your room."

What? Why would I hide a brownie in my bed? That's gross. That's messy. I like brownies, too. Plus, it's against the rules.

I tried to tell Jean that.

I tried to tell Heather that, when she came in to see what all the yelling was about.

They didn't believe me.

"You've been acting out all week, Riley," Heather said. "It would be in your best interest to tell the truth."

I *am* telling the truth! Willow isn't here on the weekends, either, so I don't even have her to stand up for me. *If* she'd stand up for me. She would, right?

They're calling Mom and Dad in for a family meeting on Monday. I wonder if this is what will finally get Dad into the hospital. Not because he wants to spend time with his daughter, but because he'll get to hear everyone talk about how much of a failure I am.

What if they kick me out? What if I have to go home without finishing treatment? I should be thrilled about that, right? I should be dancing and pumping my fist in the air. I'm not, though. It feels like someone punched me in the stomach and left a crater behind.

If I have to leave, I *know* I'll relapse. I'll stay sick forever.

Yesterday, I was determined to skip meals forever, but today it's like someone twirled me around to face the opposite direction. Behind me, there's darkness. Ahead of me is the sunrise.

I want to see the sun come up.

I want light.

I want to recover.

DAY TWENTY-ONE: SUNDAY

It's hard to focus on eating when I can't stop thinking about that brownie. How did it get there? Have I been sleeping on mushed-up chocolate for the past month?

How did Jean know to look under my bed? Food didn't just "end up" under my mattress, either. Someone put the brownie there. In group last night, every single staff member working came into the group room. They lined up in front of the couches and asked if anyone had anything to confess.

We all looked at one another. Except for me, I don't think anyone knew what was going on.

No one confessed a thing. Which means that someone's telling lies.

It's up to me to be a detective, and this will be an easy case to solve. There's only one person who has a motive for sneaking food into my room.

The person who threatened me.

The person who's actively sabotaging her own recovery.

The person who would want to sabotage mine.

Ali.

Brenna's leaving tomorrow. That's why she's been acting so weird. She found out the other day that her insurance won't pay for any more treatment and her parents can't afford the cost on their own. When she told me how much it costs to be in here, I didn't believe her at first. It's a *ton* of money.

I never used to think about things like health insurance. I went to the doctor every year for checkups. Julia went when she sprained an ankle. We saw the dentist twice a year and the eye doctor once a year. Mom, Aunt Rose, *and* Aunt Tricia all have glasses, so Mom's convinced we're going to need them, even though Julia and I have 20/20 vision every time.

Mom explained it all to me once. She has to pay something called a co-pay, and insurance pays the rest. "The rest" is usually a lot of money. That's why doctors are so rich. Why Camille and her heart surgeon parents live in a huge house with a built-in pool and a cabana. Because something as simple as an X-ray can cost hundreds of dollars. When Mom had surgery for her broken leg, it probably cost the insurance company *tens of thousands* of dollars.

I didn't cost *us* that much, though. Because insurance companies know that people need operations. That those sorts of things are necessary.

Apparently eating disorder treatment isn't necessary.

"My insurance told my parents they wouldn't pay because I'm not sick enough," Laura said. (Laura weighs practically nothing.)

"My insurance isn't paying because I'm normal weight," Aisha said. "Even though I threw up all the time and fainted in the middle of class."

Laura's and Aisha's families *can* pay for treatment, though. Brenna's family can't. Brenna's family is already struggling to pay the regular bills. Brenna's family would lose their house if they had to pay the tens of thousands of dollars to let her stay here.

TENS OF THOUSANDS!

What would happen if our insurance stopped covering my stay? Would Mom and Dad have to take out a loan? Would they have to decide between my treatment and Julia's gymnastics?

I don't think I could stand it if my parents chose some random gymnastics competitions over my life. They might. They might decide they're wasting their money if I'm still struggling so much. Dad used to ask me why I couldn't just "decide to recover." "Put your mind to it and try," he said.

I can't control this, though. I can't just make a decision and be done with everything.

I've made lots of decisions over the past few weeks. I've decided to recover over and over again, but I always get scared. I always slip back. And if I keep slipping back, then why *wouldn't* my parents give up on me? Why wouldn't they decide I'm not worth the money?

They might.

They probably should.

Brenna's worried about relapsing. She says she's not ready yet, that she's already thinking about the food that's in her pantry at home and what diet she should go on. "I don't want to think like that, but I can't help it! It's like the thoughts are a magnet. I keep pulling back, but it's stronger than me." She was almost crying. "I *know* I'll relapse if I leave. They say I'm better, but I'm not."

The counselors say that about me, too. But they don't see the mess inside my head.

"My insurance says I'm not 'sick enough' to be here now." Brenna spat the words out like they were rotten. "That since I haven't binged or purged in a month, I'm all better." She clenched her fists so tightly her knuckles turned white. "Not being at risk for death is the only thing they care about. Not that I'm scared that the second I get out of here, I'm going to get caught up in the cycle again. Riley, what if I can't do this?"

Brenna kept saying it over and over, echoing the words that tumble around my head like clothes in the washing machine: *What if I can't do this?*

I'm scared, too. I don't know what's going to happen in our family meeting tomorrow. Will Willow yell at me? Will Mom and Dad bring me home and lock me in my room forever? Will Julia disown me as her big sister?

All I could do was give Brenna a hug. I didn't have the energy to do more than that.

I didn't finish dinner tonight. My stomach hurt too much, from anger and fear and regret. I felt like I was going to barf. At least I drank the Boost. I didn't want to get in any more trouble. I didn't want Mom and Dad to be even *more* angry at me. The vanilla flavor was gross, though, like watered-down ice cream.

I should have eaten the food instead. I need to eat the food from now on.

Everyone on the staff is looking at me like I'm a criminal. I feel like Robbie Johnson in the lunchroom at school. All the lunch ladies (and the lunch man) stare at him the entire period because he started a food fight that one time. After that, he became a "troublemaker," even though he's really nice and always helps me with my math homework.

I don't like feeling like a troublemaker. I don't want to get kicked out. Every time I think about leaving, I get a pit in my stomach. It's the way I used to feel when I thought about eating dessert or skipping a run. The way I felt when I stepped on the scale and saw a higher number.

Now I feel that emptiness at the thought of being discharged.

The world is big and mean.

I'm not ready to face it yet.

DAY TWENTY-TWO: MONDAY

We had a good-bye party for Brenna today. They do it with all the patients who "graduate." She filled out her snowflake and taped it to the dining room wall. Brenna's snowflake said she was letting go of "not being enough."

I like the way she put that. It's how I feel, too. Not enough of an athlete. Not enough of a student or a friend or a daughter.

Not enough of a *me*.

We made a book for Brenna out of construction paper. It looks like the one I made in kindergarten, the one Mom still has in her keepsake box. I called it *All About Riley* and drew a picture of myself on the cover, complete with huge elephant ears and hands bigger than my head. On each page I drew a picture of something I loved:

An ice cream cone.

The *Little Mermaid* movie.

Puppies.

Nail polish.

I wonder what I'd draw today. What do I love now? Definitely not running. Every time I think about track practice, a hole opens up in my stomach. Not a hunger hole. A hatred hole, one that's bleak and lonely. I hate running. It makes me push myself until I hurt. It makes me hate myself when I don't measure up. (I never measure up.)

I'm glad I don't have to run when I leave here.

What else?

I love watching silly TV shows with Julia.

I love reading. I love action stories, but also books like *The House That Lou Built* and *Turtle in Paradise*, books with girls who don't care what other people think about them. I like those girls. I want to be friends with *them*, not with people like Talia or Camille.

I love hanging out with Emerson and Josie.

I love drawing. I love seeing what my hand can create, how I can transform reality into color and shape.

This book was for Brenna, though, one she can take with her to remember us. We each got a page where we had to write something we liked about her. I had to think for a while, because there are tons of things I love about Brenna. I doodled while I thought. I drew a wave with a surfer gliding in to shore. I drew Wonder Woman and Supergirl and Poison Ivy. I gave them different body types, one big and one small and one in-between. I drew Superman zooming into the sky.

You're strong, I wrote. *You're the strongest, bravest person I know. You are 100 percent yourself and you can do this.*

Brenna smiled at me when she read it. We hugged for a long time.

I hope she'll be okay.

And deep down, no matter how much "trouble" I make, I hope *I* can be okay, too. I hope that in our family meeting this afternoon, Mom and Dad don't yell at me. I hope they tell me how much they love me.

I hope they'll help *me* be strong and brave, too.

———

It was quiet at lunch today. Everyone kept looking at the empty seat where Brenna usually sits. There was no one talking about how Luna was so underused in the Harry Potter books or debating which of the Avengers is the strongest. No one giving us graphic novel recommendations until everyone else rolled their eyes and I told Brenna to stop until I had a pen to write down all the titles.

I ate all my food, even with Ali staring at me the whole time. The sandwich tasted dry and the chips were greasy, but I did it. One bite at a time.

Two hours until the family meeting.

———

One hour until the family meeting.

I'm drawing to pass the time, as usual. I took out the pictures

I've made of the other girls in here and lined them up on the group room table. I was planning on critiquing myself, on making a mental list of all the ways I'd messed things up.

Then Laura came over. "This looks just like me!" she said.

"Your mouth looks off, though." I wanted to grab the picture back and tear it up. Then there'd be no evidence that my drawings were anything but perfect.

"No, it looks awesome." Laura paused, staring at the picture of herself. "Do I really look like this? My body, I mean."

I wasn't sure what the right answer was, so I decided to go for the truth. "Yeah," I said. "I mean, I think you're pretty." I decided not to mention the size of her body. I didn't want to do what Ali and I used to, when we reassured each other we were still skinny. I wanted to stop focusing on our bodies, like the counselors try to do.

"This definitely isn't what I look like inside my head," said Meredith. "I look so graceful." I'd drawn her in a tutu, with a poofy skirt and satiny toe shoes.

"You *are* graceful," Aisha said. "I can't wait to see you onstage someday."

"We can all go together!" Laura laughed.

"Have you made one of you?" Aisha asked.

I blushed. There *was* a drawing of me, buried inside the pages of my drawing notebook. I drew it this morning after breakfast. It was hard to draw, maybe the hardest thing I've ever made. It felt wrong to spend so much time on myself, to think about how I looked without judging. I wanted to make every part of me smaller. Narrower. Tinier.

I tried to make it realistic, though. I tried to make it true. In the end, the picture didn't look exactly like me. But it was close. I didn't throw it away, and it didn't look hideous.

Maybe I don't look hideous, either.

Even if my drawings don't *exactly* match the images in my head, that doesn't mean I didn't do a good job. And even if I don't look *exactly* how I want to be, that doesn't mean I'm not a good person.

My drawings are unique, something only I can create.

Me.

Only me.

———

I thought therapists were supposed to be nice all the time, all reasonable and calm and "you're doing wonderful and you're amazing."

Not Willow. Not today. Today Willow only wanted to talk about what I'd done wrong. She acted like I was a juvenile delinquent who'd thrown eggs at the police station or driven a car into a house.

A kid who'd stopped eating her meal plan.

"Skipping meals, Riley?" Willow wasn't angry; she was disappointed. And that was so much worse.

"I didn't want to eat." I could have told Willow how angry I was at Mom and Dad. How I'm so scared about having no friends that my stomach is tied up in knots.

Except I couldn't get my mouth to work. I couldn't get my lips to move, even though I knew we only had a half hour together before Mom and Dad showed up. All of a sudden, I was angry again. I was angry at being confronted. At always being the one who's wrong. At Willow not taking the time to talk to me about how I *felt*, not just what I'd *done*.

"We need to talk about this, Riley. You don't want to go backward. You have so much to look forward to." Willow's hands were in her lap. She had a silver ring on her right hand. It was new and made her fingers look long and slim. I wonder if Willow likes the size of her fingers. I wonder if she likes the size of her body.

I wonder if she even cares.

"What do I have to look forward to?" I finally exclaimed. "Getting out of here and having Mom on my back about everything I eat? Emerson and Josie realizing we don't have anything in common anymore? Dad shutting me out of his life?" I didn't know why I was yelling. It was hard to breathe. My heart was fighting to escape my chest. My body wanted to escape her office. I wanted to tell Willow that I *do* want to get better, I really *do*. But the words wouldn't come.

"Life." Willow's voice was calm and even, like I wasn't freaking out in front of her, like tears weren't rolling down my cheeks and snot wasn't dripping from my nose. "You have *life* to look forward to."

"What *kind* of life?" I asked. "One where no one cares about me? Where people make fun of me?"

"Riley." Willow leaned forward. "We've talked about this before."

"I know, I know," I said. "People like me. The ones who don't shouldn't matter. Blah blah blah. I get it. I *should* know this by now. I *should* be better. But I'm not." The tears came faster. "I still don't believe everything you tell me. I still feel awful all the time!"

"You're supposed to feel awful," Willow reminded me. "Recovery isn't all rainbows and daisies."

"But you just said I should be happy."

"I want you to be happy *eventually*," Willow said. "I want you to love your body *eventually*. And you will. But it takes time. And beating yourself up for not being further in recovery will only make you feel worse."

"It does." My voice was small.

"Even 'normal' people aren't happy all the time." Willow looked at the clock. Twenty minutes until my parents showed up. "They have hard days and they cry. Normal people even dislike their bodies sometimes."

"They do?"

"They do," Willow confirmed. "But bad feelings pass. The anxiety wave rises and crests and falls. And those people move on with their day and with their life. They move on to the next happy moment. Those happy moments will come, I promise. You don't have to starve your body to numb the bad feelings anymore."

"I know," I whispered. I looked at the swirly painting on Willow's wall, the one with all the colors of the rainbow that always feels like it's sucking me in.

"I don't want to be alone."

"You won't be, Riley." Willow put her hand on my shoulder. "Your family and friends might just surprise you. And if they don't, you can handle it. You're strong. You can beat this disease."

Willow's words were a hug, wrapping me in belief and love.

"So can you explain why you skipped those meals?"

"I was upset," I said. "And sad. It made me feel better to have an empty stomach."

"*Is* empty better?" Willow held up a hand. "Take a few seconds to think about that." She leaned back in her chair and looked at the clock again. *Tick tock! Tick tock!* I could almost hear the *Jeopardy!* music in my head.

My first instinct was DUH! OF COURSE EMPTY IS GOOD. Then I realized that I've felt awful for the past few days. I've felt awful for the past year.

"It felt good *at first*. But then I felt guilty. The Boosts were gross, and skipping meals got me in trouble. It didn't make Josie and Emerson visit. It made me feel guilty. Hungry, too." I felt like I was going to cry. "I was just so angry at everyone. And I didn't hide that brownie. Really!"

I started crying again. I'm *so sick* of crying.

"It doesn't feel right anymore! Why doesn't it feel right?" I didn't know why I was crying. I didn't know if I was upset that I'd skipped meals or if I was upset that I didn't *want* to skip meals anymore. I'm so confused. Is this what getting better is like? Constantly changing my mind? Feeling guilty about feeling guilty?

"What doesn't feel right?" Willow put a hand on mine. Her hand was soft. I wanted to hold on tight. I wanted her to promise never to let go.

"Lying. Hiding. Being sick." I squeezed my eyes shut, afraid of what would come now that I'd said the words out loud. Saying them changed things. It made my decision to recover real.

It made it impossible to go back.

Willow leaned back in her chair. She smiled. I kept talking. "It's like I've been wearing a sweater for the past year. It used to be comfy and soft. It used to keep me warm and safe. It kept branches from scratching me and rain from chilling my skin."

"What's happened to that sweater now?" Willow asked.

"It's tight now. It's itchy and scratchy and doesn't fit anymore.

But not in a 'because I'm gaining weight' kind of way. It just doesn't *feel* good. It doesn't protect me."

"It gives you a rash?" Willow looked like she was suppressing a giggle. I let myself crack a tiny smile.

"An awful rash."

"You're recovering, Riley." *Willow's* smile was the biggest I'd ever seen it. "And I *do* believe you. Even if you *have* been acting out. Because that's what recovery is. Slips and falls and learning from your mistakes."

"You believe me?"

"I do." Willow nodded. "You didn't hide that brownie."

"I didn't."

Willow believed me!

"One step at a time," she said. "I'll be here to help you. And hopefully, so will your parents."

That's when I heard the knock on the door. Mom's voice in the hallway. Dad coughing.

My parents were here, but I definitely wasn't ready. Especially since they didn't even pause for a hug or a kiss or whatever signs of affection parents usually give their children.

"Why did you hide food, Riley?" Mom asked. "You were doing so well." Mom had tears in her eyes. Dad stared at his hands.

"I didn't do it." I've been repeating those same four words for the past two days. I'll keep saying them until everyone believes me. "Someone must have put the brownie there. I was framed. I know who did it, too." I felt like I was on some TV legal drama where the judge was about to bang a gavel and condemn me to life in prison. All the evidence was against me.

And to my parents, my word meant nothing.

"You're here to gain weight, Riley, not to waste this opportunity. You need to get back on track." Dad rubbed his eyes. "Do you know how much this place costs?"

Of course. Money is what matters here.

"Dad, that's not the point. You have to listen. Ali set me up. She put the food under my bed because of the whole crunches thing."

"Crunches thing?" Whoops. Mom wasn't supposed to know that part. "You're doing *crunches*? And what kind of place is this that patients can just sneak out of the dining room with food?"

"The staff is allowed to make a mistake, Mom! Maybe someone looked away for one second while Ali hid her brownie. It doesn't mean this isn't a good program."

"So you're defending this place now?" Dad looked like he was about to explode. "Of course you are; you're still skinny. You're still sick."

A thrill ran up my spine. *Still skinny! I'm still skinny!*

No! That's not what matters. What matters is getting through to my parents. What matters is making them understand that I *don't want* to be sick anymore.

Willow raised her hand. "Miranda. Nathaniel. Riley's right; we *may* have missed something. Another patient's actions were overlooked. But we're human, too. We're doing the best we can. Let's try to focus on what Riley has to say without blame."

I snorted. "Without blame. Right. That's not going to happen."

Mom stood up. "Well, what am I supposed to think, Riley? You didn't want to go out to eat with me a few days ago. Now you're hiding food and blaming other people. Where's all this progress we're supposed to be seeing?"

"Did you even hear Willow?" I asked. "I. Didn't. Do. It. Anyway, you guys don't know *what* I'm doing in here! You don't know how hard I'm working every day. How I'm eating and being honest. How I'm actually feeling better about this whole weight-gain thing."

Most of the time.

"But you're not following the rules." Dad sounded confused. He kept looking at Willow like he expected her to yell at me. In my parents' world, that's what *would* have happened. When people break the rules, they get in trouble. When they're not perfect, they're scolded.

"That means you're still sick." Mom spoke like she was the therapist, like it was *her* job to deliver the verdict on whether I'm sick or not.

In her mind, maybe I'll always be sick.

"Riley's going to be sick for a while," Willow said.

Mom and Dad smiled, like Willow was on their side. My mouth dropped open. "Hey!"

"I'm not blaming you, Riley," Willow said. "And I'm not saying you're not working hard. What I *am* saying is that you're still sick. Would you agree with me on that point?"

Well, yeah.

Willow turned to Mom and Dad again. "Recovery is a journey," she said. "It takes months, sometimes years. You can't rush it."

"Why not?" Dad grumbled under his breath. "It shouldn't be that hard." But I totally heard him. We all totally heard him.

"Recovery *is* hard." Willow looked Dad in the eye. She stared at him until he looked away. But then the *coolest* thing happened—Willow waited for Dad to make eye contact with her again, like he was some misbehaving toddler who'd drawn on the wall with crayons. She waited and waited until he finally looked up.

"Thank you," Willow said. "We *all* need to be part of this meeting for it to help you three. We *all* need to listen and learn."

"I don't need help," said Mom. "Neither does Nathaniel. Riley's the one with the problem." Mom said *problem* like I had some weird disease that turned my skin blue with pink polka dots. Like I'd grown fangs and warts and smelled like a skunk who'd bathed in rotten milk.

"I don't have a problem!" I exclaimed.

Mom raised her eyebrows. Dad sighed, that long-suffering sigh he does when someone from work texts him during dinner.

That's when I started crying. "Okay, I do have a problem. I know I have a problem. But I'm trying. I'm the *only* one trying. Mom, you won't stop dieting. Dad, you won't talk to me. My friends hate me and Ali wants to ruin my life and my head keeps spinning. I can't stop thinking and my body is growing and I don't know what's going on."

There were so many tears. So much snot. I snorted a few times, too.

Mom didn't say anything.

Dad didn't say anything.

I didn't say anything else.

"Recovery is hard." Willow's voice was soft, but we could all hear it. The only other noise in the room was the clock, counting down the minutes until my parents left me again. "Riley isn't doing this on purpose. She doesn't want to disobey the rules. She wants to recover."

"I do!" I piped up.

"Then why is she still sick?" Here's the weird part. Dad didn't sound like he was blaming me. He didn't sound like he was mad. He sounded scared, like I was one of the glass figurines Mom has on a shelf in the dining room and a light breeze would shatter me into pieces.

"Right now, Riley's brain is wired to keep her sick," Willow said. "Her body is, too. The chemicals in her head increase Riley's anxiety when she breaks her old routines and tries new things. Since her body is underweight, it's harder for her to use logic. So even though Riley's trying, parts of her are pushing back. She's going to make mistakes. That's normal."

"Normal," I echoed.

"*Riley's* not normal, though." Willow smiled at me. "Riley is extraordinary. But her journey is normal. Riley, you're not doing anything wrong. You're working and eating, and I can tell from our sessions that you have a wonderful life ahead of you."

It's nice to have *someone* believe in me.

"You guys need to try, too." It wasn't Willow saying that, though. It was me! I couldn't believe the words came out of my mouth. I imagined Mom and Dad stomping their feet and turning their backs on me. I imagined them disowning me for disrespect, packing up all my stuff and throwing it on the front lawn.

They didn't do any of those things.

"Try how?" Mom asked.

"I don't know *what* to do," Dad said.

I waited for Willow to answer, but she looked at me. "Tell them," she said.

So I told them how Mom's diets made me feel. I told them how I thought Dad hated me. I told them how I've been drawing portraits and am nervous to show them.

"But aren't I allowed to eat what I want?" Mom asked.

"I've been busy, Riley," Dad said.

"We'd never judge your art, you know that," Mom said.

I *don't* know that. Except I didn't get a chance to tell them that, because Mom started talking again.

"So you're saying this is all our fault?" Mom looked at Willow the way *I* look at Willow, like she could reach out a sturdy tree branch and save our family from drowning. Willow's not a savior, though. She's not a superhero.

That's what I've learned in here: we have to be our own superheroes.

"Mom—" I started.

"No." Mom held up a hand. "I get the whole brain-chemicals stuff. But haven't you been on medication? Aren't there groups here? There has to be a point where the excuses stop. You can't keep blaming your disease. Or your old roommate."

"I'm not blaming anyone—"

"I still don't believe you." Mom pinched the skin between her eyes. "Just last week you told me you were doing better. We had that heart-to-heart, remember? What happened?"

"Stuff happened." It wasn't much of an answer, but it was the only one I had. My parents didn't cause my eating disorder. My friends or Ali or running or the media didn't, either. I got sick because of a whole list of ingredients poured into a pot. Sometimes I can taste one ingredient more than another, but *everything* contributes, along with a few extra ingredients I can't quite identify.

I don't know exactly why I got sick. I don't know why it's so hard to get better. All I know is that I have to move forward and figure out how to turn off the flame for good.

"You don't just skip dinner because of *stuff*, Riley. You need to eat."

"I *know* I need to eat! I *am* eating!" I wanted to scream at them and pound a pillowcase. I wanted to jump inside their heads and force them to see the truth.

But here's the amazing thing: You know what I *didn't* want to do? I didn't want to run. I didn't want to skip my next meal. I didn't think about my body. I was totally focused on my parents and my anger.

I tried to explain what was happening in my head and how cool it was. Willow was proud. Mom and Dad were confused, but they at least congratulated me.

"I'm getting better," I said. "I promise. Please don't make me leave."

"You're not leaving," Dad assured me. "You need to be here."

"But can you afford to let me stay?"

I wanted them to tell me that I was worth more than all the money in the world. That I was priceless and important and they'd never give up on me.

"We're okay as long as insurance is paying, honey," Mom said. "You just need to get better. Stop lying. Stop breaking the rules."

"I'm not lying. I didn't hide that brownie. Why won't you believe me? Willow does!"

"Willow doesn't know you like we do. And Riley, you've lied to us a lot." Mom said it gently, but her words burrowed under my skin like pointy, accusing needles.

Poke. Poke. Poke.

My parents are never going to change. They say they want me to get better. They say they love me. But they're never going to change.

—

"Why'd you do it?" Ali and I were alone in the group room. The other girls were waiting for the bathroom, and Ali was engrossed in her book. I had to pee super badly, but it was the first chance I'd had to confront her. We weren't alone at night anymore, and the counselors usually trailed her like the stink of BO follows the boys in my grade.

Now, though, it was just me and her. I could tell she wasn't reading, either. She'd been on the same page *forever*.

"Why'd I do what?" Ali's voice was laced with innocence, but the fake kind, the kind that oozes off Talia when she "compliments" me on my outfit:

"Wow! That shirt actually doesn't make your arms look big."

"Nice skinny jeans. You're totally brave to wear them."

I always stayed silent, even though what I wanted more than anything was to confront Talia or call her a jerk.

I was always too chicken to do that. I'm not chicken anymore, though.

"You hid food underneath my mattress. You got me in trouble." I forced my voice not to tremble. It's a good thing I have the very best willpower in the whole wide world.

"I didn't." Ali looked down at her book again. She turned the page. She was such a faker.

"You did. You're the only one who was mad at me. It had to be you."

"So what are you now, a detective? Little Miss Nancy Drew? Do you need a magnifying glass and a trench coat?"

"Whatever." I turned around in my chair. I'd given Ali a chance to explain. To prove that, deep down, she did bad things because she was struggling. Because she was haunted by the same ghosts that visited me so often. But she still wanted to shut me out. She still wanted to be sick.

I can't break through that brick wall. I know that from experience.

Then I heard Ali crying. First soft sobs, so quiet I thought it was the trees rustling outside. Then louder, the choking sobs I've cried so often myself.

"I don't know why I did it," she sobbed. "I was so afraid you'd tell on me about the crunches. Then I was so mad you *did* tell. So I did what I've done with *my* food a few times. But this time I put it in a different place. And I told Jean it was you." Ali glared at me. "Now they won't leave me alone. I have to follow all the rules."

"You have to *recover*, you mean?"

Ugh. I sounded like a Goody-Two-shoes. I sounded as annoying as I thought everyone else did when I first got here. But we *should* follow the rules, right? As hard as it is, we *do* have to recover.

"You sounded like you were going to die."

"I wasn't going to die." Ali rolled her eyes. "Everyone says I'm going to die, but I'm not."

"Why don't you believe them?"

"Because."

"That's not an answer."

I knew what Ali meant, though, because I feel the same way. Yeah, I know eating disorders kill people, but I never think that could happen to *me*. I'm not a statistic. I'm stronger than my hunger. I'm invincible. I thought of Brenna and her superheroes again.

"We all have Kryptonite, you know." I said it softly, more like I was talking to myself than to Ali.

"I don't even know what that means." Ali sniffled a whole bunch more. "You're so weird."

I didn't take it as an insult, though. Today, I'm reclaiming *weird* as a compliment. Because weird doesn't always have to be bad. Weird just means different, and different can be good.

Different means that I'm me.

"Don't do it again," I told Ali. I don't know if I sounded fierce or if she'd really learned something, because she answered right away.

"I won't. Never again."

DAY TWENTY-THREE: TUESDAY

I miss Brenna.

I miss Emerson.

I miss Josie.

I can't call Brenna, and I'm too scared to call my friends, so I called Julia instead.

Her voice bubbled through the line when she answered. She sounded tired, but the bubbles were still there. The bubbles are always there with Julia. "Mom let me download this cool game on her phone with magical panda bears and unicorns and there's this awesome quest to find a buried treasure. It's hard, but I'm so good already. I'll show you when I see you next. Can I visit—"

I cut her off. "I love you."

"Huh?"

"I love you. I wanted to tell you that. And I'm sorry."

"Sorry about what? What do you mean?"

For being jealous.

For hating you.

For making you worry.

I didn't say any of those things, though. "I'll be home soon," I said. "I'm working hard."

"I know you are. Oooh! Guess what I did at practice today for the first time?"

"Oooh, what?" I listened. I was excited. I was a good older sister.

I'll *be* a good older sister.

———

Mom and Dad came to visit tonight. They brought a jigsaw puzzle, one of those five-hundred-piece ones with the smallest pieces in the world. The box had a picture of Cape Cod on it, with a wave breaking and a crab scuttling along the shore and a lighthouse shining from the end of a jetty.

I think a few pieces were missing, and then we kept losing more on the floor. We talked about the new guy at Dad's work who snaps his gum super loudly and the exhibit Mom saw at some gallery across town: "Lots of modern stuff," Mom said. "Bright colors. Reclaimed junk." She peeked at me. "I saw some pictures of unicorns, like you used to draw. Some portraits, too."

She said she liked them. She said the artist was talented.

I think that was Mom's way of apologizing. Of being her own version of a lighthouse, shining a beacon for us to see by.

DAY TWENTY-FIVE: THURSDAY

Willow told me to make a list of reasons I want to recover. It sounded cheesy at first (everything here sounds cheesy at first), but I think it'll help. She told me to look at it anytime I'm having trouble. Anytime I feel anxious or like I want to give up and control my body forever.

I'm going to try to believe that a silly list can help me get better. I guess that's all I can do, right?

RILEY'S REASONS FOR RECOVERY
(It has a nice ring to it!)

1. I can be on the track team again. Not now, but eventually. If I want to.
2. I can go to sleepovers and parties without worrying about food.
3. I can eat pizza and ice cream again.
4. It won't hurt to sit in a chair without a cushion.
5. I won't be cold all the time.

6. Emerson and Josie won't get mad at me for canceling plans.
7. Dillon and Tyler won't call me "Skinny Bones" and "Skeletor" anymore.
8. I won't think about food all the time. I can think about school and homework and get good grades again.
9. I won't be tired every minute of every day.
10. I'll be able to fall asleep.
11. Mom will be proud of me. (I think.)
12. *I* will be proud of me. (I know.)

———

RILEY'S REASONS TO STAY SICK
(Willow didn't ask me to make this list, but I did it anyway.
It's shorter than I expected.)

1. I'll still be skinny.
2. Talia and the other kids at school won't make fun of my body.

It's not that long. It's not that impressive.

DAY TWENTY-SIX: FRIDAY

I'm so sick of wearing hospital gowns. They're ugly and stained and don't even cover my butt. I try not to think about where those stains came from. And why the hospital won't buy new ones. I just put them on, step onto the scale backward, and close my eyes, holding on to the fabric the whole time so the world doesn't see my behind.

I don't want to know what I weigh anymore. Isn't that weird? That number used to be the most important thing in the world to me. Some people need coffee to function in the morning. I needed to know my weight.

I still care, of course. I think I'll always care. I'll always wonder. But I don't want to *know* now.

I'm afraid of what I'll do when I see that high number, whatever it is. What if it scares me and I start hating myself again?

I don't want to hate myself anymore.

—

I've been eating all my meals. All my snacks, too. I *do* want to eat and I *don't* want to eat, both at the same time. I feel proud and guilty, both at the same time. I feel like two different people in the same body.

When I was a kid and Mom read me stories before bed, we always did four stories—I chose two and she chose two. That way, even if Mom groaned when I chose *Corduroy* for the five zillionth time, she still had to read it.

Mom always wanted to read this boring book about a little girl with a devil on one shoulder and an angel on the other. The book wasn't that good. It was one of those books that are supposed to teach kids a lesson, where the devil and the angel told the girl different things to do. I thought it was silly when I was five, but now that I'm twelve it makes more sense.

Right now, the devil is poking his pitchfork into my shoulder. He's whispering that I don't need food, that I'm stronger than my body, smarter than anyone else.

The angel is brushing her soft feathers against my cheek, cooing that I'm brave and powerful. That I can beat this disease.

When I was sick, I listened to the devil every time. His voice is softer now, but he's still poking me. His pitchfork is still pointy. He's trying to draw blood.

I'm listening to the angel, though.

I feel full and gross, but the devil is getting quieter.

Willow says that's how I know I'm doing the right thing.

DAY TWENTY-NINE: MONDAY

Brenna's back. She got here this morning after breakfast. We were all in the group room, doing some worksheet Heather passed out about self-soothing techniques (A warm bath! Cuddling with a cat! Smelling flowers!), when Meredith elbowed me in the ribs.

"Ow!" Meredith's pointy elbow hurt. I bet I'm going to have a bruise tomorrow. Then I looked up and saw Brenna. She was outside the group room window. Her shoulders were slumped, her eyes red.

Her dad was with her. I recognized him from when she was discharged, when he came in for her good-bye party and to help her pack up her stuff. He's way tall, with a potbelly and a bushy beard. Snippets of his voice came through the thin walls:

". . . do it this time . . . one more shot . . . no other choice . . ."

I shouldn't have been listening, but I couldn't exactly turn him off. He was loud. Everyone was staring. Everyone was listening. Heather switched on the TV. "Nature shows can be soothing, too!" She made us watch an old episode of *Planet Earth*, one with screeching birds and roaring lions. TV didn't soothe *me* at all, though.

I keep thinking about how Brenna looked when she'd left, so shaky and afraid. She knew she wasn't ready. She was right.

Now she's back. A repeat customer, just like Aisha. Just like me someday?

No, *not* like me.

How *do* I recover? I've been here for a million years now. I've shoved food—lots of food—down my throat. They've taught me "life lessons" and "coping skills." I should feel like a better person now, right? A person who cares more about friends and school and life than my body.

Except I *still* feel like the same old Riley. I still think about my body.

I still feel like a fake.

———

Josie sent me a letter!!!!!!! That deserves seven exclamation points. That deserves seven *million* exclamation points. This journal is definitely not big enough for that, though.

Riley,

I'm sorry I got mad. I'm sorry you got sick. Emerson told me you're doing better. I hope you can come back to school soon.

My birthday wasn't that much fun without you. No one could agree on a movie to watch, and all the songs I picked for the dance party seemed babyish. Chloe kept asking why I hadn't invited boys—umm, because I didn't want to? Because all the boys in our class are super annoying?

Talia got glasses last week. They're these big black frames that she says are "way stylish" and "the latest thing." Except I'm not sure Talia really needs them to see, because she doesn't wear them half the time. Now all the other girls are wearing fake glasses, too. It's really weird.

Talia asked how you were doing the other day, like I would know the answer. Usually I would know the answer. I used to know everything about you. I'm not sure if Talia was looking for a reason to make fun of us some more or if she really cared. Either way, I care. I'm not that mad anymore. Even if you messed up, I still want you to be my friend.

I hope it's not too scary in there. I hope you know that I love you and that you're awesome.

Love,
Josie

!!!

I didn't feel guilty after lunch today! I ate the food and tasted the food. Everything tasted *good*, too! I went to our next group and drew and read some of my book. Then all of a sudden I realized I hadn't thought about lunch once.

It felt like someone had let me out of a jail cell after I'd been sentenced to life in prison, except instead of my body, it was my brain that was free. I wasn't cooped up in an endless circle of *I ate something bad. I'm so bad. I have to fix this.*

Things were different. My race car *stopped* going around and around the track. It got on the exit ramp. I *thought* different things, too. I thought about how when I got out of here, it would be fun to bake cookies with my friends. How maybe if I stopped biting my nails, Mom might take me with her to get a manicure.

How the sky looked really pretty and I wanted to draw it.

How my latest portrait of myself looked . . . kind of nice?

How lately, I want to draw way more than I want to run.

Then I had snack.

And . . . now I feel guilty for eating.

Baby steps, right?

DAY THIRTY-ONE: WEDNESDAY

I think I'm doing better. I know I'm doing better. So why does the scale still freak me out? Why am I still afraid of a silly number?

I asked Willow that today. I told her how this morning's number is haunting me, how I'm afraid that if I see it, I'll backslide. I told her how weighing myself used to be the first thing I did every morning and how if the number was higher than the day before, my mood was ruined.

If the number was lower, I was happy. Elated. Overjoyed. I was every synonym in the thesaurus. But only for about ten minutes. Then I started worrying about what would happen if I gained weight the next day.

"Then why use the scale?"

"We *have* to get weighed in here," I pointed out.

"Yes," Willow agreed. "Because we're making sure you get to a healthy weight range. That's our responsibility. *Your* responsibility is to lessen the power that number has over you."

Willow's right. The scale is like a magnet, pulling my body and my mind to it. I remember how the morning of our class trip to the amusement park, I weighed more than the day before.

While everyone else was having fun on the Ferris wheel and going on the Corkscrew roller coaster seven times in a row, I was moping and obsessing.

I remember getting on the scale last month and losing a whole pound in a day. Before I stepped on the scale, I was upset. I'd gotten a 70 percent on my math quiz, way lower than my usual scores. I was tired and cranky and still had to read five chapters for Language Arts *and* go for another run.

Then I saw the number. The *lower* number.

I felt like I'd won the lottery. I felt like I could lift a car over my head or bend a steel bar in my hands. The anxiety and exhaustion slid off me like a snakeskin, coiling on the floor by my feet. My new skin was relief. Power. Invincibility.

Then, after a few minutes—even a few *seconds*—the snakeskin started to grow back. It covered me from head to toe, thicker than before. Harder to shed than before.

My next thoughts always came quickly:

I could get that number lower.

I should get that number lower.

If I'm not careful, I'll gain it back.

I never let myself rest. I always had to go for the next run, skip the next meal. I never reached the finish line.

Willow pulled a scale out from under her desk. It was old and black. My heart did a double beat in my chest. I had to get weighed *again?*

"What would happen if you stepped on this and you saw a high number?"

I'd have failed.

I'd be fat.

The world would be over.

I shrugged.

"What would happen if you saw a low number?"

"I'd win."

Willow cocked her head to the side. "You'd win what?"

I thought for a few seconds. "When I get on the scale and the number is lower, I feel like I can take over the world." I peeked at Willow. She didn't look disgusted. "I feel like I'm powerful. Like I'm the *best* at something and no one can take that away from me."

"It makes you feel good," Willow echoed. "It makes you feel in control of your life when it's spinning out of control."

"Yeah."

"Does it make you feel bad, too?"

"All the time."

"More than it makes you feel good?"

"Yeah," I admitted. "I hate the scale. I hate how it makes me skip parties because cake would make the number go up. I hate how it makes me sad when everyone else is happy. I hate how I can't stop thinking about how every single thing I do will affect it and how it keeps calling me names."

"The scale is a machine," Willow said. "An appliance, like a microwave or a blender. It's something human beings crafted and put together. Something that can be taken apart." She pulled open her bottom desk drawer and took out a different scale, this one in pieces. I stared at them: The cracked window where the numbers appear. The inner workings, shiny and metal, strewn over her desk. The red needle and the circle filled with numbers that somehow define who I am.

Parts.

That's all the scale was: a broken collection of parts.

It wasn't human. It wasn't real.

It didn't have power over me.

It *shouldn't* have power over me.

DAY THIRTY-TWO: THURSDAY

I miss my friends.

I want to go home.

———

"We have the bestest, most amazing, most super-fantastic, unbelievable-istic news in the history of EVER!" That's what Emerson screeched when she burst into my room at the start of visiting hours. Josie was behind her. Heather was behind *them*, shushing Emerson.

I laughed. My heart beat faster in my chest. I had *just* written about how much I missed my friends. Is my journal magical? Can it grant my wishes? Obviously not, but I'll take this magic any day.

"I'm sorry." That's what Emerson said next. "When I visited, I saw that really skinny girl and started worrying you were going to die. I thought something I'd say might make you worse so then I was super rude and mean and then I felt so guilty that I was afraid you'd be mad if I tried to visit again and oh my god, I'm sorry." Emerson took a deep breath.

Josie pretended she was Emerson collapsing from oxygen deprivation. Then she inched closer to my bed like I was a snake about to bite her. "I'm sorry, too. You got my letter, right?"

"I did." I hugged her. "It's okay. I'm sorry, three." I looked at Emerson. "I'm not going to die."

I looked at Josie. "I'm not going to skip any more parties."

Silence for a few seconds. Then another screech from Emerson. "The news!"

I thought she was going to tell me her aunt Isabelle visited from Paris again and brought her the most "*très chic*" hat ever. (Even though we both look ridiculous in hats. Especially berets.)

That Josie had finally gotten a higher grade than Lola Lopez on the spelling test.

That (a total long shot) Tommy Bell had asked Emerson to the Winter Wonderland dance.

No. It was *even better*. Emerson's dad got tickets to an art show in Boston. (*That* part wasn't a big deal. I've been to tons of Mom's shows. When Mom first got her job, Julia and I had to dress up for all her opening nights. We wore fancy scratchy dresses, said hi to all Mom's coworkers, and then had to leave before the desserts came out. Fancy art shows are no fun.)

This was an art show for adults *and* kids, though!

"There will be adults displaying their stuff, but also real artists teaching classes for kids *our age*," Emerson said. "There will be demonstrations on watercolors and oils and sculpture and even graphic novels! Plus, you can enter a raffle to have some famous guy look at your work. How cool would that be?" Emerson ran out of breath again.

"You could get discovered!" Josie bounced on my bed. It squeaked, reminding me of the noise it made when I used to do crunches.

I feel different than that girl. I *am* different than that girl.

I still wanted to say no, though. It was like how I used to automatically say no every time anyone asked me to hang out. I couldn't go to the mall. I couldn't go to the movies. I couldn't go to a sleepover. If I did, someone would discover my secret. I wouldn't be able to exercise. I'd have to eat.

Now, my reasons are different, but that urge to flee is the same. What if I *do* win that raffle? What if I show my work and get confirmation that I'm awful?

You're a fraud.

You don't deserve to put your art into the world.

Stay small.

That's what the voice in my head tells me.

That's what I pushed back against.

"Of course I want to come!" I forced the words out. Because deep down, I *want* to go to the art show. Deep down, I'm more excited than scared.

"Awesome! The show is next Saturday night and Mom and

Dad said they could drive us all. And maybe if you get discharged in time, we can still do that art class? It starts in a few weeks." Emerson looked at the ground and shuffled her feet, like she was afraid I was going to say no.

"I'd *love* to do that art class! Maybe I *will* be discharged by then." For the first time, I really believed that life "outside" could be different. It could be good.

"Do you want to see my portraits?" Without hesitating, I showed my best friends a bunch of my sketches. Not just the ones of the other patients, but also the ones I drew of myself.

They said they were good! They didn't say they were awful! I think they were proud of me, too. It was the best feeling ever.

Then I realized the *worst* thing ever.

"Wait. The show is next weekend? I can't go."

"What? No!"

"I haven't been approved for an overnight pass yet, and Boston is far enough from the hospital that I'd probably have to sleep at home." I wanted to cry. I wanted to have fun with my friends and learn from famous artists who didn't know my mother. I wanted one night away from here, one night of vacation from my eating disorder.

Emerson and Josie begged me to ask.

"You have to come!"

"It won't be the same without you!"

Even if I don't get approved for a pass, at least now I know that my friends still want me around. That I have friends to go back to when I recover.

Not if.

When.

———

Willow says she'll have to talk to the treatment team. "We might be able to get you a twenty-four-hour pass," she said. "You can go to the art show and sleep at home. It'll be good for you to try out life on the outside. To use your coping skills and come back to talk about how it goes."

I felt like doing a happy dance. That might be considered exercise, though, and I have to be on my *best* behavior now. I wonder if I'll have to present my case to the people in charge of the hospital. I'll dress up in a pantsuit and pack a briefcase and act all lawyerlike. I'll shout "Objection!" when they bring up the brownie incident and pace in front of the jury as I argue how much better I am.

I practiced that argument with Willow.

"Here's what I'd say: 'It may just be an art show, but it's an experience, too. It's something I can share with my best friends that will make me feel normal. It's a way to develop my interests and plan for my future.'" I smiled all toothily like I was posing for a camera.

"What about the food?" Willow asked. "You'll be going out to dinner, right?"

I stopped smiling as that familiar pit of fear opened up in my stomach. The deep, dark pit I always get stuck in. Then I remembered that I can climb out of that pit now. They've given me tools to use. Ropes and ladders and pickaxes. Assertiveness training and self-esteem class and positive self-talk.

"I'll eat dinner," I said. "My friends will help me. I'll pick out a restaurant and look at the menu online. We'll figure out what fits in my meal plan. It'll be okay."

It really feels like it'll be okay, too. It's just food. I've been eating for weeks now. I can totally eat around my friends. They won't judge me. Maybe we'll even get frozen yogurt afterward. Or ice cream! (I think I can do that.) As long as Emerson and Josie don't make a big deal out of me eating. That'd be embarrassing.

I'll sleep at home. I'll wake up in my own bed and have breakfast and hang out with Julia and relax and *oh my God I have to eat breakfast with my parents and try to "relax" around Dad and I can't go for a run how I am supposed to do that I can't do this ahhhhhh!*

I'm breathing really fast right now. My pulse is bumpety-bumping like a train rattling at top speed, when the scenery flashes by and the floor vibrates and everything turns into a blur. My *life* is a blur right now.

It's less blurry than before, but the colors still run together. There are still moments of swirling black and white and muddy brown, still moments when I can't tell exactly what I'm seeing. I can walk forward, though. I can walk one step at a time, slowly, until I get more practice seeing the world in this new way.

I can do this. I'll follow my meal plan and then come back and tell everyone how awesome it went and how recovered I am.

I'll be amazing.

DAY THIRTY-THREE: FRIDAY

Brenna's curled up in the corner of the couch, her earbuds stuffed in her ears, her eyes closed. She's been so sad ever since she came back. I keep trying to talk to her about what happened, but she ignores me every time.

"What happened to you?" I whispered. I didn't mean for her to overhear, but she did. I was glad she did. I needed to know where she'd gone wrong. I needed to know so I could do things right.

Brenna's eyes opened. "It's hard out there." Her eyelids closed again, but I couldn't hear her music anymore. I knew she was listening.

"I thought you were going to get better?" I asked. "I thought we were both going to."

"I didn't do this on purpose, Riley." Brenna sat up. Her fists were clenched, her voice loud. "Relapsing doesn't make me bad, either. I just . . . it's hard out there. And I wasn't strong enough." Tears ran down her face. "There's so much to deal with."

I imagined a giant obstacle course, except instead of climbing walls and pits of fire, there were moms on diets or friends complaining about their clothing size. Instead of balance beams and rope swings, there were tight-fitting clothes and a world that denied us the freedom to live in our own bodies.

"I started a diet," Brenna said. "Just a little one, because someone at school made fun of me. I thought that maybe if I lost weight, things would be better. People would like me."

"I like you," I said.

"No one else does." Brenna laughed, but it was a sour laugh, full of lemon and vinegar. "Even that girl I danced with laughed at me. I thought we were friends. Then, after a few days of dieting, I was hungry. So I ate. I ate to spite all those awful people in school and I ate to spite myself. Because I'll never get better. Never ever ever."

"You *will* get better." The words sounded hollow. I could knock on them and hear the echo for a million years.

Because I don't know if Brenna will get better.

I don't know if I will, either.

I'll try, though. I'll learn from Brenna and plan for the hard stuff. I'll wish on stars, but I'll also do the work.

I will get better.

———

I GET TO GO TO THE ART SHOW NEXT WEEKEND!

I'm leaving the hospital for a whole twenty-four hours!

I get to sleep in my own bed and spend time with my friends and eat nonhospital food!

We had another family meeting this afternoon. Well, Willow and I had a meeting with Mom. Dad had something to do at work. I don't know if I believe that, but I'm trying. I don't want to be angry at anyone right now. Mom says that as long as I give her my meal plan in advance, I can come home.

Home!

DAY THIRTY-SIX: MONDAY

In morning group today, we talked about death. Not in a morbid way; more in a "how do you want to be remembered?" way. I don't like thinking about death, but Heather made us all talk. The funny thing is, group actually made me feel better.

"What do you want written on your tombstone?" Heather leaned forward, like she was trying to stare into our souls. I crossed my arms over my stomach, like my soul was hanging out in there with my partially digested breakfast.

"'Here lies Ali'?" Ali finally said. "'She lived a long, long life.'"

"'Laura lived to be one hundred and twenty.'"

"Let's go a little deeper." Heather adjusted her glasses. I may not like Heather, but I *do* like her glasses. They're blue with gold polka dots. I wonder if Talia would approve of Heather's frames.

"Some people have 'Beloved Mother' written on their tombstone," Heather said. "Or 'Friend.' 'Dear Wife.' Some people have their occupations. Their passions. 'Writer.' 'Engineer.' 'Dog lover.' Some people's just say their name.

"What do *you* want written on your tombstone?" Heather asked again. "'She was skinny'? 'She spent her life on a diet'? 'She could have been an astronaut, the president, a concert singer, a mother, a friend . . . except she spent too much time counting fat grams'?"

We talked about what our eating disorder is stopping us from doing. We talked about who we can be without it. It made me realize something: every second of every day, no matter what I weigh, my life is going by.

I don't want to waste one more second of it.

Here Lies Riley Logan, aged 102.

She lived a long, happy, and healthy life.

She was a good friend.

She was good at art. She might not have been the greatest ever, but she worked hard.

She listened and learned.

She liked to read.

She was a nice sister.

Everyone liked to be around her, because she made them feel better.

She was funny.

Those would be nice things to have on my tombstone.

DAY THIRTY-EIGHT: WEDNESDAY

To-Do List Before I Leave on Pass:

- ☐ Go over meal plan with Caroline.
- ☐ Make a list of "expected obstacles" with Willow.
- ☐ Pack.
- ☐ Draw a lot. Pick out my best portraits in case I win the raffle.
- ☐ Calm down, because I don't know if I can make it until Saturday night!

DAY FORTY-ONE: SATURDAY

Willow says I can do this, but I feel like a baby getting ready to take her first steps. Emerson and Josie say they'll help me if I wobble, but I'm the one who's going to fall flat on her face, not them.

I don't want to crawl forever, though. It's only going to hold me back.

I can learn to walk.

Then I can learn to fly.

We're in the restaurant now. This place is super dark. There are lamps over every table, but they're dim and the rest of the restaurant is all shadowy. I don't know how the waiters deliver their orders without tripping over something. Maybe they'll drop my food and I won't have to eat it. That'd be a great excuse for skipping dinner.

No! I don't want to skip dinner. I have to eat dinner. I'm normal. Normal people eat at restaurants. They like eating at restaurants. I can totally be normal. Yep. Normal Riley, that's me.

Emerson and Josie are in the bathroom now. Josie drank three cans of Diet Coke this afternoon and this is the second time she's peed since we got here. She ordered another one when we got here. I had to order regular Coke.

I'm proud *and* annoyed at myself. I didn't *have* to order regular soda. Emerson and Josie don't know the rules, and no one at the hospital would ever find out. Even Emerson's parents, who are sitting at a table across the room, don't know about my meal plan.

I know, though.

My eating disorder voice is really loud out here. It's like I was wearing headphones in the hospital—the chatter wasn't silenced, but it *was* muffled. Now the world is turned to full volume.

There's an entire section on the menu called "Skinnylicious," which is pretty much the dumbest thing ever. I don't want to be *anything-licious.* It's all diet food and there are calories listed next to each option and I'm pretty much freaking out right now.

I forced myself to tell Emerson and Josie that I was nervous, that my brain was trying to convince me to change the meal order I had planned.

Emerson shrugged. "Then change your order. I bet everything tastes good." Emerson doesn't know what's going on in my head, though. She doesn't see the mental calculator adding up the numbers, comparing one choice to another. She doesn't see the gears spinning so fast that all my logic and planning is going up in smoke. I don't care about the *taste.* I care about the fact that I can't

231

stop seeing those Skinnylicious calories in my head, even though I turned the page. They'll be there forever, like the Sharpie unicorn I drew on the kitchen wall when I was six.

Then Josie surprised me. "You planned something with your nutritionist, right?"

I nodded. I knew that if I talked, I'd cry.

"Is it on the menu?"

I nodded again. I pointed to the third page. "There."

"Then order that."

It sounded so simple. Maybe it *was* so simple.

"Do you want me to order it, too?" Josie asked.

Maybe Josie *does* understand. Well, as much as anyone without an eating disorder can understand.

"You don't have to." She *shouldn't* have to. I know that I need to learn how to eat in the real world. I know that people won't always be ordering the same meals as me.

"I want to," Josie said.

"And if *we* eat it, you'll know it's okay," Emerson said. "Yummy, too!"

I felt like a baby, but maybe I *am* a baby when it comes to eating. At least I don't have to eat pureed carrots.

We all ordered from the non-Skinnylicious menu. And you know what? It *was* yummy.

—

Emerson and Josie wanted to dress up for tonight, even though we had no idea what the dress code was. Or what professional artists wear. They could wear funky T-shirts with pictures of superheroes on them or satin ball gowns with stilettos. We went for something in-between.

"Skirts!" Emerson pulled a bunch out of her closet. Mom had dropped me off right from the hospital, after making me promise a billion times that I'd "follow the rules."

"Dresses, too!" Josie had brought some of her clothes over. Mom had packed up some of my old stuff, too.

"We need to look older. Professional."

Josie nodded. "So the famous people take us seriously."

I didn't want to dress up, but they convinced me with squeals and music and an impromptu dance party. With makeup, too. I took it off right after I looked in the mirror, though. I had so much eye shadow on that I looked like a purple raccoon. I felt fake.

I don't want to be fake anymore.

What I *wanted* to do was wear my sweatpants and fuzzy socks, like I've been doing for the last two months. I didn't want to try to squeeze into my old clothes. I knew nothing would fit, and I was right. My favorite dress was too tight in the hips. None of my jeans zipped or buttoned. My shirts squeezed me like a hug. I ended up borrowing something of Josie's. Her clothes didn't feel strange, either. They fit. They were comfortable. They were right for my new body. I felt confident.

So why am I hiding in a bathroom stall right now? Why did I run out of the art show?

I told Emerson and Josie I had to pee. I almost asked them for permission. Then when I *did* pee, I had to stop myself from counting out loud. I would have totally scared the lady in the stall next to me. She's gone now, though. She washed her hands and left. I'm still here. It's quiet and peaceful, even if it does smell like that gross lemon air freshener that gives me a headache.

There are so many people out there. Kids with perfect posture who strut around like they've won every award in the world. Kids with cool clothes who probably sweat creativity. Adults with shiny shoes and pictures hung in shiny frames. There are signs pointing to ceramics classes upstairs and still-life classes downstairs, acrylics down one wing and metalwork down another.

I want to try everything.

I want to hand my portfolio to every teacher who walks by.

I want to hide my portfolio forever.

We pooled our money so I could buy twenty entries into the raffle. I want to win, but what if it turns out that I'm talentless and pathetic? I'd have to give up drawing then, and I *need* to draw. It's the one thing that makes me feel normal. It's the only thing I have left.

DAY FORTY-TWO: SUNDAY

Home.

My bedroom's the same. Same purple-and-yellow flowered comforter. Same collection of photos thumbtacked to my bulletin board. Same Lumpy McLumpykins propped against my pillow. I hugged him right away. I really should have brought him to treatment. I thought the other girls would laugh at a stuffed koala bear, but Ali has her stuffed monkey, Mr. Goober, and Meredith has a platypus.

Mom's making breakfast downstairs. I smelled it the second my alarm went off. Willow told me to set it for seven, so I wouldn't sleep through breakfast. I have to eat three meals at home today. Two snacks, too. (I'll be back at the hospital for evening snack.)

I smell pancakes and bacon. I haven't had either in ages. My chest feels tight every time I think about eating breakfast with my family. What if they stare at me the whole time? What if I eat too much? What if Mom does that thing she used to do where she smears butter all over my food and hopes I don't notice?

She's not supposed to do that now. I'm supposed to be responsible for myself.

I *proved* I can do that last night. I even got frozen yogurt after the art show—I ordered a small cup and ate it all, even though the portion size was massive. It was yummy and I wanted more. So I ate more. I listened to my body. It was pretty cool. (*Skinnylicious* is still a ridiculous word, though.)

I proved I could ignore my eating disorder. Because that's who I realized was talking to me in that bathroom. Ed (or whatever that voice is) had disguised his voice to sound like me. I let down my guard. I forgot for a second that I'm an awesome person and a good artist. That I have friends.

I didn't 100 percent believe all that stuff, but I *told* myself it was true. Like Brenna tells (told?) herself that she's happy. Then I marched out of the bathroom and joined my friends. People smiled at me. Other kids talked to me and I learned tons of new stuff, stuff that I might want to *keep* learning about.

Last night I didn't worry. Last night I ate. This morning is different, though. This morning I'm afraid of eating with my family. I'm afraid of what they'll do. Of what they won't do.

There's a big breakfast waiting for me downstairs, like a present I didn't ask for. Like a package of underwear or a stocking full of coal. I keep telling myself things will be okay, but I don't believe a word of it. I have a meal plan to follow, but I don't want to follow it.

Mom just yelled up. Time to go downstairs.

Help.

"I thought this was your favorite breakfast." Mom's fork hovered over her plate. Julia and Dad had taken three pancakes each, slathered butter on them, and dumped a bucketful of syrup on top. Mom had taken two and left them naked, then decorated her plate with strawberries and blueberries. I did the same.

It was apparently the wrong move.

"It *is* my favorite breakfast." I pointed to my plate. "I'm eating it." I'd even asked for a yogurt for extra protein. I followed my meal plan exactly, but that wasn't enough for Mom.

"You don't want more than two pancakes? I made extra to make today special." Mom bit her lip. Julia looked up with that "oh boy, here we go again" expression on her face. Dad kept stuffing food into *his* face.

"It *is* special." I started cutting up my pancakes. "You're eating two, too. I'm fine."

"Let me see your meal plan again." Mom put her hand out.

I shook my head. "I already showed you." Mom looked at it so long last night I thought she was cramming for a test. And I *knew* Caroline had e-mailed it to her. My mother didn't need to see it again. Not here. Not *while* I was eating.

"Don't you need butter? Are you skipping your fats group?" Mom's voice rose, like I was a teenager who'd stayed out past curfew.

"Mom! I was just about to ask for it."

I think I was. Yeah, I totally was going to ask for the butter on my own. I would have. Really. I only needed a certain amount, though, so I asked Mom for the measuring spoons. That's what was on my meal plan. No more and no less. I asked her for the measuring cups, too, for the syrup.

Dad finally looked up. "This again, Riley?" He sighed. "Just dump on some syrup. It's not going to kill you."

It is going to kill me.

No, it's not. It's just butter. Just syrup.

It's sugar and fat and calories and you're going to get sooooooo fat.

No, I'm not. Being fat isn't a bad thing anyway.

Plus, Caroline said this breakfast is fine.

She said so. But she could be lying.

The voices in my head roared to life, sending me onto the highway of self-doubt. Pinpricks of fear danced across my skin. I wanted to run away, but I tried deep breathing instead. *In, out. In, out.*

"I can't 'dump on syrup,' Dad. I have a meal plan."

"I don't think they'll care if you eat more." Dad laughed, like everything was a big joke. Like he hadn't been in the family meeting when Willow said how hard recovery was.

Maybe recovery *is* a big joke to them. Because Mom and Dad aren't changing. At least Julia is acting normally. She even skipped gymnastics this morning to spend time with me.

"Recovery isn't something I can improvise, Dad. I need structure first. I need to get my food confidence back." That's what

Willow told me. That's why after discharge I'll have therapist and nutritionist and doctor's appointments all the time. Why I have to make a daily schedule for myself. It's like in musicals: actors need weeks and weeks of rehearsals with the script before they can do the show on their own. They need practice before opening night.

I definitely don't know my lines yet.

"We'll help you, right, Julia? Food is good!" Mom took a bite of a strawberry. A really small bite. Then a sip of her water. Her noncaloric water.

Julia's eyes darted between us. "Sure." Her face sent me a silent apology.

"I need the measuring cups and spoons," I repeated.

"But I thought you were better now." Mom's voice was a whisper.

I didn't meet Mom's eyes. I looked out the window instead. At the garden bed in the side yard. At the black squirrel running across our yard, the one who comes back every year. At the fence Julia and I had painted when we were little. Dad didn't trust us with real paint, so he'd given us paintbrushes and cans full of milk, so our mistakes wouldn't matter.

They didn't trust me with paint back then. They don't trust me with food now.

Maybe they never will.

The thought made me want to cry. It made me want to throw the jug of syrup against the wall and watch the sticky syrup drip onto the floor. That's when I realized the truth: My parents may *never* see me as recovered. They might *always* see me through disease-shaded glasses.

"Maybe I'm *not* better." I shoved my plate away and ran up the stairs.

"Riley! Come back here now. You have to eat! Riley!" Mom's words trailed me like a puppy dog yapping at my heels, but I didn't go back down.

I'm not going back down.

—

I don't know what to say to Mom anymore. She thinks that recovery is the only thing we should talk about. Doesn't she understand that I'm still Riley? I'm more Riley *now* than I was before. I want to talk about drawing and what I'll be doing at school for the rest of the year. I want to talk about what movies I want to see and how old Mr. Tanner down the street dyed his white hair green. I saw him walking his dog and did a double take. Julia and I laughed for about ten minutes straight. She snort-laughed *twice* in a row.

Julia's talking to me normally, at least. We watched a bunch of movies this morning and shared popcorn and juice for a snack. She didn't mention my body once. She asked about my friends at the hospital. (Mom winced when Julia called them that.) She told me her best friend, Grace, got a pet pig and showed me pictures. It's a way cute pig.

But every time Julia distracts me, Mom jumps in and accuses me of doing or saying or feeling something wrong. She makes me *feel* wrong. Until I came back home, I thought I was doing better. But if I am, why couldn't I eat breakfast? The second they let me out of the hospital, I screwed up.

I looked down on Brenna for not trying hard enough, but here I am, too. Proving that I'm still sick, too.

My room is the way it was before. The creak of the floor and the cars driving by outside sound the way they did before. I guess *I'm* the way I was before, too.

I want to go back to the hospital. Where they make the decisions for me. Where people understand how my brain works. Where my sick self belongs.

DAY FORTY-THREE: MONDAY

I didn't confess about the pancakes until halfway through my session with Willow. I didn't want to say *anything*, but the secret was a lump in my throat, cutting off my air supply and choking me.

"I freaked out at breakfast yesterday. I didn't eat anything. Not even a bite." I squeezed my eyes together like a little kid playing hide-and-seek. If I couldn't see Willow, she couldn't see me. She couldn't tell me what a failure I was.

Instead, she told me she was glad.

"Good. I was waiting for that slip." Willow was about to say something else, but I interrupted her.

"You were waiting for me to fail? Was everyone taking bets? Putting money into a jar to see when poor Riley would do something wrong? You don't believe in me that much?" I felt like a snowball rolling down a hill, picking up speed and anger by the second.

"Whoa, hold on!" Willow held up a hand. Her white shirt had a sweat stain under her right armpit. I stared at it. The stain was really obvious. Why hadn't Willow noticed it when she'd gotten dressed? Had anyone else noticed and not told her? Would she smell if I got closer?

I'd way rather think about smelly armpits than about how much of a failure I am.

"That's not what I meant." Willow didn't sound mad. Was she faking it? She *had* to be faking it. She had to be mad.

"Then what did you mean?" I asked. "Why did you expect me to relapse?"

"You didn't relapse, Riley. You slipped. There's a big difference."

Then, as usual, Willow went on to be her super-smart, super-capable, super-annoyingly right-all-the-time self. And as usual, I listened and learned and tried to become a better person.

(I'm noticing a pattern.)

Apparently slips are one-time things, like skipping a meal. Running an extra mile or weighing myself. Slips are something I can come back from. Mistakes I can learn from.

"That's why I'm glad you had a slip while you were at home," Willow said. "Because now we can analyze why you got upset at breakfast and what you can do in the future when those same triggers come up. Because they will, again and again. And if we can't figure out *how* to change your reactions, *that's* when you'll relapse. That's when you won't be able to pull yourself back from the edge."

I pictured myself teetering at the edge of the Grand Canyon, my arms windmilling in the air, a bunch of pointy rocks below me.

I don't want to relapse.

So I worked with Willow. I was more honest than I've ever been.

I told her about how it felt like Mom was forcing food on me. How even though I had fun with my friends, I feel like a stranger in my own life. How Dad spent all Sunday morning in the basement fixing his bike. I didn't even know he had a bike. Maybe he started a new hobby while I've been away. Maybe he rides his bike every single day now and it's his one true passion. Maybe not, though. I bet he was trying to avoid me.

Then I told Willow how Dad gave me a hug when he dropped me off and told me he was proud of me. How I showed Mom one of my drawings and she said it was good. How awesome Emerson and Josie were at dinner, and how I'd forced myself to go back in to the art show.

"Failures *and* successes," Willow said. "I'd say you had a fabulous pass overall."

Maybe I did.

We figured out a plan then: How I can speak my mind in the future and who to reach out to when I'm anxious. How to block out the unhelpful stuff Mom and Dad do and focus on what *I* need to do instead. How I'll have a therapist and a nutritionist when I leave here who'll listen to me, just like Willow does now.

How I'm *allowed* to make mistakes. How it doesn't mean I'm weak. How it doesn't mean Brenna was a failure. How it's part of the process and that with every struggle I overcome, I'll get stronger.

How the bad body image won't last forever.

I laughed at that last one. It seems impossible that I'll ever be happy with my body.

"It *is* possible." Willow's lips curled into a smile. Her eyes twinkled. "Take it from me."

I'm not sure what Willow meant by that. She didn't say anything else, and when I pressed her for more, she told me our time was up.

I think Willow might mean that *she's* recovered.

That *she's* proof that recovery is possible.

Cool.

DAY FORTY-SEVEN: FRIDAY

I *really* have to be strong now. Because it's my turn to be discharged.

They told me this morning. We'd just finished art therapy and I had colored chalk all over my black yoga pants. I'm basically only wearing yoga pants now. Those and leggings. Anything with an elastic waistband. That way I don't have to suck in my stomach while I try to fasten a button that doesn't want to be fastened. I don't have to feel the rough fabric of jeans rubbing against my oversize thighs. I don't have to *think* about the concept of *skinny jeans*.

I still miss my skinny jeans. I miss a lot about before, but I'm trying to remember that I'll be getting so much more in the future.

Now the future is a lot closer than I thought it'd be.

The doctor in charge of the program told me I'm not leaving because of insurance. I'm not leaving because I got in trouble. I'm leaving because they think I'm better.

Better.

It's a single word, but it holds a dictionary full of meanings:

Better means I don't worry about my weight.

Better means I don't worry about Talia making fun of me.

Better means I don't worry at all.

I worry *all the time*. So how can I be better?

Willow said it's okay to worry. She said my fears are perfectly normal and I'm still on a journey. It feels like I've been on a journey *forever*, but I guess she's right. I may have to travel further, but at least I've started.

I keep trying to wipe the chalk off my pants, but it's not all going away. It's smudged in there, a faint cloud against the black fabric. There's a snag in the fabric, too, one I'm picking at every few seconds. The thread is unraveling. Now there's a hole.

I've worn these pants a lot. I probably need new ones. I probably need a whole new wardrobe. Clothes to fit my new body.

Clothes to fit the new me.

DAY FORTY-EIGHT: SATURDAY

I have five days left. They kick you out fast around here.

Today Mom took me out on pass to visit with a therapist near our house. I had to tell the new lady all about me and Julia's gymnastics and Talia's mayonnaise crusade and even Ali and the brownies. (Ali and the Brownies. That's my next band name.)

I told her about what I used to do and what I'm afraid of. I talked so much I bet I'll have no voice tomorrow.

Dr. Silverman was okay. She's young, with chin-length hair and a tattoo of a laurel wreath on her ankle. She had a cup of cherry lollipops on her desk, like it was a pediatrician's office, and even though I felt like a little kid taking one, I still did. I like lollipops. And cherry is my favorite.

Dr. Silverman (she told me to call her Margaret, but I kept forgetting) had one of those fountain thingies on her desk, the kind with pebbles and running water. I had to pee *so* badly by the end of my session. ~~Dr.~~ Margaret let me go by *myself*, though, *and* I didn't have to count. She treated me like an actual *person*.

So did Mom. In the car, we talked about school and how excited (*really!*) I am to do schoolwork again. We talked about how annoyed Mom was that none of her friends from book club ever read the book.

"They want to gossip the whole time!" Mom threw up her hands, then quickly put them back on the steering wheel. "I mean, I like to talk, but I like talking about books, too! Can't we have a balance?" I giggled. Mom giggled.

Maybe *we* can have a balance, too.

DAY FORTY-NINE: SUNDAY

We got a new patient today. Her name's Olivia and she's from
New York City. She's wearing fancy designer jeans that make
her legs look like matchsticks and has a shiny purse that probably cost more than Mom's and Dad's cars combined. The purse
is orange and reminds me of the plastic pumpkins we take
trick-or-treating.

Jean took the purse right away, though, like she took my
phone when I got here. Olivia protested for like five minutes.
I wonder if I used to sound like that.

Olivia sounds annoying.

She sounds scared.

I want to give her a hug and tell her it's going to be okay. I
want to tell her that they might seem mean here, but they really
want to help. That she's going to hurt at first, but she'll feel better
soon.

When I *tried* to talk to Olivia, though, she wrinkled her nose
like I smelled bad. Which I *don't*. I took a shower and put on body
spray this morning, the same as any other day. I smell like soap
and vanilla. Then Olivia looked me up and down and put her fin-

gers on her chin like she was a fancy art critic appraising a new acquisition. Like Mom does when she's cultivating her gallery.

Maybe Olivia hates the way I look.

Maybe she doesn't like my body.

For a few seconds, I started hating my body, too.

Then I remembered the cool thing about art: everyone likes different styles. There's a place out there for every type of art. It all belongs somewhere. I may never have my portraits displayed in Mom's gallery, but they might end up in another one someday. Especially when I get better at art.

Especially when I get *better*.

Mom doesn't have to display my art to like it.

I don't have to win awards to keep drawing.

My pictures belong, just like I belong.

I hope Olivia learns that she belongs, too.

I drew a picture of Olivia this afternoon. I added a superhero cape and gave it to her after snack. She raised her eyebrows. "What's this for?"

"To remind you of what you can do," I said.

Brenna looked at the superhero and smiled. I smiled back.

DAY FIFTY: MONDAY

Three days left.

Mom and I visited a nutritionist today: Stephanie. *She* had tubs of plastic food, too. And a scale. Two scales, actually: one for food and one for me. The scale for me was one of those old-fashioned ones they have at the doctor's office, where you have to slide the tab back and forth until the scale balances. I wonder if she'll make me get on it all the time. I wonder if she'll tell me my weight.

I don't want her to.

I do want her to.

I wonder how much I've gained.

Mom and I went out for lunch before she took me back to the hospital. When we got to the restaurant, Dad and Julia were there. Dad had skipped work and dismissed Julia from school so we could have a family lunch.

Mom didn't order a salad, either. And she got a regular soda. I gaped at her.

"Don't just stare, Riley. Put some food in that mouth." Mom was smiling, though. She was making a joke!

Before I would have started crying. I would have acted all offended and stormed off.

Today I laughed. I ate my sandwich. I listened to Dad talk about the *five* deer he'd seen on his bike ride to work this morning. (Huh. Maybe he *is* into biking now.) I listened to Julia talk about how annoying it is that she can't go on the team trip to Six Flags. Because Mom and Dad are spending money on me instead? I don't know. All I know is that Mom changed the subject. She asked me a question instead of talking about gymnastics. Then Dad asked me another one.

"I'm okay." I whispered it to myself at the end of the meal, when I finished my last sip of milk and wiped my mouth. "I'm going to be okay."

Mom overheard me. "Of course you are, honey." She squeezed my hand. "Smooth sailing from here on out, right?"

Mom still doesn't get how hard this is going to be. She might *never* get it. But maybe she doesn't have to.

She's not me. I'm not her.

I'm not Talia or Julia or Josie or Emerson.

I'm Riley.

Riley's pretty awesome.

DAY FIFTY-ONE: TUESDAY

Two days left. I can't do this. Not on my own. I'm not strong enough.

What if I forget that it's okay to gain weight? What if I start thinking that fat is bad, even though I know it's not? What if the world turns up the volume on its "skinny is beautiful" messages and I forget that loud doesn't equal true?

What if I forget how to love myself?

I keep tapping my foot and wiggling around. How could anyone think I'm "better"?

I'm a total fraud.

DAY FIFTY-TWO: WEDNESDAY

One day left. When I got here almost two months ago, a week sounded like an eternity. A day sounded like forever. A minute seemed like too much to endure. I've been here for fifty-two days now. That's almost a full term in school. That's almost a full track season.

That's 1/7 of a year, almost 1/84 of my life.

I feel like I just got here, though, like I just walked in the door with Mom. Like I just met Ali, asleep in the bed next to me. Except she was just IV Girl then. She hadn't betrayed me yet.

I hadn't met Brenna.

Josie still hated me and Julia was the Gold Medal Daughter.

I was skinny then. I was scared.

I'm not as skinny now, but I *am* still scared. But it's a different kind of scared. Just like now I'm a different kind of strong.

Instead of being scared of what *could* happen and probably won't, I'm scared of what I *know* will happen. That's why I'm making a plan about how to deal with everything. We talked about it in our family meeting today, when Mom and Dad came to meet with me and Willow.

Willow told them how hard I've been working.

Willow told them she was proud of me. I waited for Mom to say she was proud of me, too, but she was checking her voice mail. Her *voice mail!* In the middle of a family meeting *right before my discharge!* My chest tightened. My fists clenched. My stomach rolled.

I took a deep breath, though, and told Mom how she was making me feel. Willow stopped Dad before he could tell me I was being disrespectful. I didn't cry, and Mom apologized. She said she was waiting for a call from the gallery. The basement had flooded and she'd left before the plumber showed up. My mad transformed to grateful like Clark Kent stepping out of a phone booth. Mom left a gallery emergency for me. That's a big deal.

It's also a big deal that I didn't jump to conclusions. Progress!

I think having Willow there helped all of us not get so upset at one another. Willow won't be at home, though. That's where my relapse prevention plan comes in. We typed it up and signed it and everything. It has stuff like who I can reach out to for help and what my warning signs are.

It looks fancy. We're going to hang it on the fridge.

Now I just have to follow it.

DAY FIFTY-THREE: THURSDAY

One last weigh-in.

One last vitals check.

One last breakfast.

One last meeting with Willow.

She cried. I cried. We hugged. I wondered if she could feel the new fat on my stomach, the layer that covered my body like a snowsuit, but I pushed the thought away.

Snowsuits are warm and comfy. My snowsuit fits me perfectly.

Willow says she believes in me. She says I'm strong and capable and smart and funny. She says the world had better watch out, because I'm coming for it. Willow's a cheeseball.

(I love her for being a cheeseball.)

One last group, which turned into a going-away party for me. The other girls made streamers, like we did for Willow's party. They drew a picture of a cake on poster board and hung it on the wall. We played "Pin the Candle on the Cake" with stickers. I did awful. I've always been bad at that game. When I was seven, I almost walked into the pool at a birthday party.

I hugged Brenna. "I'll miss you," I said. "I'll miss our talks. I'll miss your comics recommendations."

She giggled and handed me a piece of paper. "Oh, I have a whole list here for you to try. Because I'm not going to see you for a while. You're going to beat this. You're not going to come back."

"She's not." Aisha stuck her head between us. Her eyes sparkled behind her glasses. "I know it's hard not to copy me, since I'm so awesome, but you need to try."

I stuck my tongue out at her and laughed. "It'll be tough, but I'll do my best."

Brenna wasn't laughing. "Do it for us. Because we couldn't." The words trembled in the air like a baby bird learning to fly.

"You'll do it, too," I said. "You both will."

I'm going to miss Brenna. I'm going to miss everyone. I never thought I'd make friends in here. I never thought it'd be less than 100 percent awful.

I never thought that it would change my life. That it would change me.

Aisha just shrugged. "Maybe I can do it. We'll see."

I'm never going to act like that. "We'll see" won't get me through the lunchroom. It won't make me eat my meals when Talia decides pizza is evil or I get frustrated that I'm not a better artist.

"We'll see" can't be my armor.

I will *do this.*

I have to do this.

There's no way I'm not going to do this.

Those will be my sword and my shield, the words I turn to when I teeter and totter and falter and almost fall.

I'm going to do this.

I am strong. Stronger. Strongest.

Brenna told me we have to stay in touch. Everyone else said that, too (except Olivia, who is still *way* too cool for me), but Brenna's the only one I really want to keep in my life. I'm glad to say good-bye to Ali. I understand her more now, but I still don't want to see her again.

I think talking to everyone else would remind me of how sick I used to be. I don't want that reminder. I want the present and the future, not the past.

My family is picking me up in an hour. Mom wants to go out for a celebratory dinner. Last night on the phone, Dad suggested an all-you-can-eat buffet.

"Dad." I heard Julia in the background. "Seriously? No way." Julia has my back, just like I have hers.

I might be ready for a buffet eventually, but not now.

Baby steps.

Sometimes infant steps, as long as I'm moving forward.

I don't have to be Skinny Riley anymore. I don't have to change my body.

I can be a new Riley, a Riley who draws and works on her

art and sleeps late and rests. A Riley who'll probably go out for ice cream tonight, not frozen yogurt. I may even eat the whole thing again, too.

I'm going to see Emerson and Josie tomorrow. We're going to the aquarium. It's a little-kid thing to do, but I'm excited. I love the penguins there, *and* we get to touch real starfish! Josie suggested it because it's not focused on food.

I love her for that. I love both of my best friends. Emerson promised she'll sign up for the next community art class with me since I wasn't discharged in time for the first one. Josie promised she'll help me catch up in my classes. Emerson said she'll yell at Talia for me. I told her to beat Talia in a race instead.

My plan is to ignore Talia. I'm going to try, at least. I still don't know how I'll deal with the comments on Monday. About how "healthy" I look. How much I've changed. How I'm eating "sooooo much food."

This is going to be hard. These last two *months* have been hard, though, and I made it through.

We're going into the dining room in a few minutes, and for me, it's not just a final meal. It's time for me to fill out my Elsa snowflake, to tell the world (or at least the hospital) what I'm going to let go of. I've thought about it all week. I filled out snowflakes in my mind and crumpled them up. I've *dreamed* of snowflakes.

When I first came here, I couldn't imagine my name being on that wall. I couldn't imagine being someone who was *actually* leaving this place, someone who *wanted* to let go of her eating disorder.

But I do.

I wish I could tape more than one snowflake up there, because I have a whole whirling winter wonderland of things to let go of. I finally narrowed it down to one snowflake, with a design as unique as me: *I let go of fear.*

Fear of the world.

Fear of being unlovable.

Fear of weight.

Fear of taking up space.

Fear of being *Riley.*

It's okay to be Riley.

I want to be Riley.

I am Riley.

AUTHOR'S NOTE

I was diagnosed with an eating disorder when I was eighteen years old: *anorexia nervosa* with accompanying exercise addiction, much like Riley. My issues with food and self-esteem started much earlier than that, though. They started in seventh grade, when I started worrying about fitting in and began comparing my body to the bodies of my peers.

I was a lot like Riley. I worried that I wasn't as "pretty as," "smart as," "athletic as," "skinny as," and on and on and on. When I started getting sick and losing weight, I got attention. I finally started feeling special. What years of illness and ultimately recovery taught me was that having an eating disorder is not what made me special. Yes, it got me attention at first, but it was the wrong kind of attention. It was attention that I received because people were worried about me. Through therapy and eating (yes, eating! Proper nutrition helps your brain function and helps you see reason and logic) and lots of learning and reflection, I started to realize that I didn't *have* to be the smartest or the skinniest or the *best* at anything.

All I had to do was be myself. Being myself was good enough.

If you want to read more about my journey to recovery, along with tips for navigating your own struggles, I also wrote *You Are Enough: Your Guide to Body Image and Eating Disorder Recovery.*

Remember: recovery is possible. If you are dealing with body image issues or think you might have an eating disorder, the following two organizations are a great place to start:

National Eating Disorders Association:
nationaleatingdisorders.org/help-support

**National Association of Anorexia Nervosa
and Associated Disorders:**
anad.org/get-help

ACKNOWLEDGMENTS

This book has been in my head for years. This book took me so many false starts to begin. In so many ways, *Good Enough* is me. Riley is me. So thank you, reader, for reading. Thank you for letting Riley's story into your minds and your hearts. If you are struggling with an eating disorder yourself, thank you for fighting. Thank you for pushing back against the "never enough" culture we are steeped in. Thank you for being you.

My deepest gratitude to my editors, Jean Feiwel, Christine Barcellona, and Val Otarod, whose insight, intellect, and sensitivity helped to shape this book. Your feedback was always spot-on, and you helped make Riley and her peers into fully formed people.

Thank you to Brianne Johnson, my amazing agent, whose energy and enthusiasm for this business, for writing, and for story buoys me. Bri, you are such a great advocate, cheerleader, and friend, and I'm so glad to have you by my side.

So many thanks to the amazing team at Macmillan Children's and Feiwel & Friends, who helped with so many aspects of this book. Kelsey Marrujo, you are a force of nature, and I'm so grateful to have you as my publicist. I am so honored to work with the talented Liz Dresner, who did the amazing cover and interior design, and with Romy Blümel, who did the cover art and perfectly captured the eyes that Riley feels are on her. More thanks to Melissa Zar, my amazing marketing talent; Jessica White, who proofread this manuscript; Bethany Reis, eagle-eye copy editor; Raymond Ernesto Colón, production manager; and Alexei Esikoff, managing editor.

No one should travel this publishing and writing journey alone, and I am incredibly lucky to have the Electric Eighteens group behind me for advice, laughs, and commiseration. Cindy Baldwin, Jenn Bishop, Cory Eckert, and Pam Styles read early drafts of this book and sent me valuable feedback. Sarah Hollowell did a much-appreciated sensitivity read on this manuscript, and I thank her for her time and valuable feedback. Rachel Simon was there every step of the way and is my sounding board, a cheerleader, and a friend. Katherine Applegate, thank you for your support and kindness.

A huge hug to my best friends, Kate Averett, Jena DiPinto, and Pam Styles, who are there every second of the day and night, listen to every neurotic thought in my head, and shower me with love. You girls are my forever sisters.

Thank you to the teachers and librarians who have embraced and recommended *P.S. I Miss You*, especially Erica Redner-Danzig. People like you, who encourage a culture of learning and literacy and help place the right book in a student's hand, will help to change the world. Thank you to my readers, for embracing Evie and embracing me.

Thank you to my family for a lifetime of support, encouragement, and love. I am so lucky to have you—I don't have enough pages to name you all but you are in my heart.

An immense note of gratitude to the staff of Walden Behavioral Care and Laurel Hill Inn, especially Linda McDonald and Tenley Prince. You helped me navigate my own recovery and I would not be here without all of you.

Above all, thank you to my amazing husband, Brian, and my daughters, Ellie and Lucy. I am so proud to be a writer, but I am even prouder to be a wife and a mom. Brian, you are my best friend and you never stop convincing me that I am enough. You three challenge me, support me, and fill my life with love, laughter, and silliness. Everything I went through led me here, and I couldn't be more grateful.

If you liked

GOOD ENOUGH,

don't miss these other titles
by Jen Petro-Roy!